Nancy Mitford

Wigs on the Green

Nancy Mitford, daughter of Lord and Lady Redesdale and the eldest of the six legendary Mitford sisters, was born in 1904 and educated at home on the family estate in Oxfordshire. She made her debut in London and soon became one of the bright young things of the 1920s, a close friend of Henry Green, Evelyn Waugh, John Betjeman, and their circle. A beauty and a wit, she began writing for magazines and writing novels while she was still in her twenties. In all, she wrote eight novels as well as biographies of Madame de Pompadour, Voltaire, Louis XIV, and Frederick the Great. She died in 1973. More information can be found at www.nancymitford.com.

Nancy Mitford

Wigs on the Green

Introduction by Charlotte Mosley

Vintage Books
A Division of Random House, Inc.
New York

FIRST VINTAGE BOOKS EDITION, AUGUST 2010

Library of Congress Cataloging-in-Publication Data

Mitford, Nancy, 1904-1973.
Wigs on the green / by Nancy Mitford; introduction by Charlotte Mosley. —
1st Vintage Books ed.
p. cm.
Originally published: London : T. Butterworth, 1935.
ISBN 978-0-307-74085-4 (pbk.)
1. Sisters—Fiction. I. Title.
PR6025.I88W54 2010
823'.912—dc22
2010021931

www.vintagebooks.com

Printed in the United States of America
10 9 8 7 6 5 4 3 2 1

To Peter

'That man is by nature a buffoon and that his best work is done in an antic, is a theory which gentlemen of leisure and high spirits will find very comforting.'

A. F. WEDGWOOD.

Introduction

Wigs on the Green, originally published in 1935, is Nancy Mitford's third novel. Like its predecessors, it is a light, accomplished comedy of manners, complete with Wodehousian conventions of a rich heiress, rivals in love, legacies from an aunt, broken engagements, assumed identities and a happy ending. But unlike her other books, *Wigs on the Green* was never reprinted during Nancy's lifetime.[1] In the three years following the publication of her second novel, *Christmas Pudding*, her own world and the world beyond had become less carefree places. Hitler was in absolute power in Germany and two of her sisters, Diana and Unity, had attended a Nazi Party rally at Nuremberg and become his fervent admirers. When Nancy's publisher begged her to be allowed to reissue the novel in 1951, she refused. 'Too much has happened for jokes about Nazis to be regarded as funny or as anything but the worst of taste,' she wrote to Evelyn Waugh, 'so that is out.'

As in all her books, Nancy drew freely on family and friends for inspiration and *Wigs on the Green*, despite its opening disclaimer that the characters are drawn from imagination, is closely auto-biographical. Captain Jack, the leader of the Union Jackshirts (a precursor of P. G. Wodehouse's farcical aspiring dictator Roderick Spode, leader of the Black Shorts) is modelled on Diana's lover and future husband, Sir Oswald Mosley, founder of the British Union of Fascists. Eugenia Malmains, the rebellious heiress and Jackshirt enthusiast, is a thinly disguised portrait of Unity, who moved to Munich in 1934 to learn German and fulfil her ambition

---

[1] An American mass-market paperback, the only post-war edition of *Wigs on the Green*, was published in 1976 in a single volume with Nancy's first novel, *Highland Fling* (1931).

of meeting Hitler. Nancy's distaste for republishing – just six years after the end of the war – a book that poked fun at Fascism and sent up Hitler is understandable, but it was not the only reason why she was reluctant to see the novel back in print.

Nancy's first two books had pigeonholed her as a lightweight novelist of the cocktail party/country-house weekend/society gossip-column variety. *Highland Fling* was recognized by *The Times Literary Supplement* for its 'infectious gaiety', and *Christmas Pudding* praised for keeping the reader 'laughing through its pages', but the same newspaper gave *Wigs on the Green* a disparaging review, describing it as an 'extravaganza' in which the humour was 'too clumsy to achieve the desired result.' Nancy was under no illusion that her pre-war novels were masterpieces ('*Christmas Pudding* is pathetic, badly written, facetious & *awful*,' she wrote – exaggeratedly – to Evelyn Waugh), but she also knew that they had value as period pieces, were very good entertainment and extremely funny in parts. It was not professional pride, therefore, that decided her against reissuing *Wigs on the Green*. The main reason for her refusal, apart from the jokes about Nazis, was that the book had caused such furious reactions within the Mitford family: Unity threatened never to speak to her again and Diana, who had recently divorced her first husband for Mosley, more or less broke off relations until the end of the war. Added to this, no doubt, was Nancy's unwillingness to revive the memory of Unity's suicide attempt in 1939 and her consequent death in 1948.

A consummate tease, Nancy could never take politics, or indeed anything, very seriously. Her way of dealing with life was to treat everything, on the surface at least, as a huge joke. As the eldest of the six Mitford sisters, she had communicated this attitude to her siblings and it pervaded the family atmosphere. The earnestness with which Diana, Unity and the fifth sister, Jessica – who became a Communist – embraced extreme politics broke the unwritten Mitford code that nothing was too important not to be laughed at. Nancy also had an instinctive distrust of ideologies. 'There isn't a pin to put between Nazis & Bolshies, if one is a Jew one prefers one & if an aristocrat the other that's all as far as I can see. *Fiends*,' she wrote to a family friend at the outbreak of war. Politics for Nancy came down to personalities; people, not ideas, were what counted. When she turned from fiction to writing about French history, she was accused by historians of retelling tales of Mitford family life. 'Very true,' she wrote to Jessica, 'History is always subjective & the books we yawn over are often the descriptions of the home life of some dreary old professors.'

In spite of its references to the politics of the day, *Wigs on the Green* is above all an exploration of love and marriage – themes to which Nancy returned in all her books – and it is dedicated to her husband, Peter Rodd, renegade son of the diplomat Sir Rennell Rodd. When she began writing it, in spring 1934, she had been married to Peter for just a few months; long enough, however, to take a cynical view of marriage: 'It's such a fearful gamble. Much better put your money on a horse and be out of your misery at once,' says Jasper Aspect, the unscrupulous, heavy-drinking womaniser whose character owes a great deal to Peter and, to a lesser extent, Basil Murray, his Oxford contemporary. (The raffish pair had already served as the inspiration for Basil Seal, Evelyn Waugh's delinquent anti-hero in *Black Mischief*.) Nancy and Peter rushed into marriage in a whirlwind of euphoria. Peter was nearing thirty and seems to have regarded matrimony as a last resort, having failed in everything else. He was no doubt fond of Nancy in his way but treated her, like all his women, callously, and enjoyed boasting to his friends that he had proposed to all sorts of women and that she was the only one 'fool enough' to accept him. At twenty-nine – an age when unmarried women were getting on for being old maids in the 1930s – Nancy was on the rebound from an affair that had limped on for four years with Hamish Erskine, a homosexual friend of her brother, and she fell for Peter's insolent, tow-headed charm.

An eternal romantic despite her merciless wit, Nancy willed herself to be in love and managed to shut her eyes to Peter's true character for the six months they were engaged, writing to a friend that she was in a 'haze of insane happiness' and urging everybody to get married if they wanted 'a receipt for absolute bliss'. Perhaps the p.s. in her letter, 'Please excuse these lunatic ravings', hints that at some level she recognized that marrying Peter was madness. By the time they got back from honeymoon, the romance had fizzled out. They began married life in a small house in Strand-on-the-Green, Chiswick, subsisting on a slender allowance from both sets of parents and the money that Nancy could scrape together from writing.

Nancy grew up at a time when marriage was virtually the only career open to women of her background. A marriage must be kept going at any cost and a wife should defer to her husband. The example of the Mitfords' parents, Lord and Lady Redesdale, was deeply instilled in their children in this respect. In *Wigs on the Green* Nancy takes a clear-eyed, sardonic look at her predicament. 'These vague romantic impulses won't do anybody any good, and least of all yourself,' Poppy St Julien remarks briskly to Lady Marjorie Merrith, who has broken off her engagement to the Duke of Dartford because she is not in love. 'There are times, my dear old boy,' Jasper Aspect lectures the fortune-hunting Noel Foster, 'when love has got to take its proper place as an unethical and anti-social emotion.' Nancy is trying, not always convincingly but with a notable lack of ill humour, to set aside disappointment and get down to the business of being married. When Jasper disparages the 'precious little poppet' who likes to have 'a nice long cosy chat' on the telephone in the morning, Nancy is ridiculing her love of chatting, her favourite form of intimacy. There is something almost admiring in her oblique references to Peter's financial irresponsibility: 'Wives aren't expected to keep their husbands,' says Poppy. 'I never could see why not. It seems so unfair,' Jasper replies. When Poppy points out that it is the least men can do when women go through all the trouble of pregnancy, Jasper retorts, 'Well, us boys have hang overs don't we? Comes to the same thing in the end.'

If Peter's reaction to being portrayed by his wife as a wastrel and a cad – however engaging – went unrecorded, Diana and

Unity's response to Nancy's satire did not. Diana met Oswald Mosley in early 1932, when she was twenty-one and had been married to Bryan Guinness, heir to a brewing fortune, for three years. Mosley, a Conservative, Independent then, briefly, Labour MP, had broken with mainstream politics and was preparing to launch the British Union of Fascists. He was persuaded that the existing system of government could not deal with the severe economic and social problems caused by the Great Depression, and believed that a movement, organised along paramilitary lines, was needed to take control of the economy and combat the inevitable rise of Communism. Putting his followers into military-style uniform and modelling himself on Mussolini's brand of Fascism, Mosley seemed to Diana to have all the answers to Britain's woes. That he was married and a notorious philanderer did not prevent her from falling deeply in love. By the end of the year she had asked Bryan for a divorce and moved into her own house in Eaton Square, London. When Mosley's wife died in 1933, Diana became his *maîtresse en titre* and married him three years later. Her conversion to his ideas was immediate and lifelong; like a tiger protecting its cub, she would leap to her beloved Leader's defence whenever he was under attack.

Initially, Nancy hoped that *Wigs on the Green* would amuse Diana, who seemed not to have minded a caricature of Mosley in 'The Old Ladies', an unpublished story she wrote in 1933 in which the 'Little Leader' was cast as a figure of fun who visited the old ladies 'armed only with two revolvers, a bowie-knife and a bar of Ex Lax, the delicious chocolate laxative'. The first indication that *Wigs on the Green* might cause real trouble came when Nancy had already written more than half of it. In November 1934, Mosley won a libel suit against the *Daily News* for an article published in the *Star* and was awarded £5,000 in damages. Peter Rodd was worried that he might take legal action against Nancy, who could not afford to fight a case and desperately needed royalties from the book. Nancy quickly wrote a placating letter to Diana, promising to let her edit the novel before publication and assuring her that even though it contained 'one or two jokes' it was very pro-Fascism. Diana was not mollified. The BUF was losing support; its militaristic, anti-Semitic stance was discrediting it in the eyes of the public, and its image had been badly damaged by the violence that broke out between Blackshirts and anti-Fascist hecklers at the infamous Olympia rally in June 1934. The idea that her sister might in any way harm Mosley's reputation infuriated Diana. Nancy refused to abandon the book but she did agree to remove nearly everything directly relating to Captain Jack – some three chapters altogether. Shortly before publication, she sent Diana another cajoling letter, attempting to justify her position, 'Honestly, if I thought it could set the Leader back by so much as half an hour I would have scrapped it, or indeed never written it in the first place . . . I still maintain that it is far more in favour of Fascism than otherwise. Far the nicest character in the book is a Fascist, the others all become much nicer as soon as they have joined up. But I also know your point of view, that Fascism is something too serious to be dealt with in a funny book at all. Surely that is a little unreasonable?'

Diana was not appeased. She froze Nancy out of her life for several years and never invited her to Wootton Lodge, the house in Staffordshire where the Mosleys lived between 1936 and 1940. When Diana was imprisoned in Holloway for three-and-a-half years during the war – under Defence Regulation 18B, which allowed the government to hold without charge anyone suspected of Nazi sympathies – her letters and visitors were restricted. Nancy wrote to her half-a-dozen times and did go to visit her, but relations only really began to thaw after the Mosleys were released and Nancy went to stay with them to finish *The Pursuit of Love*. The two sisters never referred to *Wigs on the Green* again in their voluminous correspondence, or indeed discussed the war or politics – subjects that would have made reconciliation difficult. Diana found out only after Nancy's death that in 1940 she had denounced her to the Foreign Office as 'a far more dangerous character' than Mosley and had urged that she be put in prison. And she never found out that Nancy had protested against her release in 1943, claiming that she was 'wildly ambitious, a ruthless and shrewd egotist, a devoted Fascist and admirer of Hitler'. Had Diana known, reconciliation would no doubt have been impossible.

The disparaging references to divorce that are sprinkled throughout *Wigs on the Green* must also have irritated Diana. Eugenia Malmains' grandmother, Lady Chalford – an adumbration of Lady Redesdale – deems the death of her son from wounds received the day before the Armistice a lesser disaster that the fact of his divorce, and regards with horror 'the tainted blood of an adulteress' that Eugenia carries in her veins. Nancy did not approve of Diana leaving Bryan but had supported her decision. The Redesdales, however, were appalled, particularly by the fact that it was Diana who petitioned Bryan for divorce on the grounds of adultery. At the time, it was common for a man to assume the role of the 'guilty party' and arrange to be caught at a seaside hotel with a tart, but Diana's parents thought it wrong and were deeply shocked that she should go along with it it.

Diana's reaction to the publication of *Wigs on the Green* affected not only the two sisters' relationship, but also eradicated any of Nancy and Peter's pro-Fascist leanings. 'I hope', Unity wrote to Diana in November 1934, 'that that utter swine Peter has resigned his membership *publicly*.' Nancy, having considered herself a Socialist, joined the BUF soon after she married, partly because Peter was initially enthusiastic about the movement and partly, no doubt, to support Diana. The two sisters had grown particularly close during the year before Nancy married, when Diana lent her a room at Eaton Square and they had seen a great deal of each other. Nancy and Peter had attended the Olympia meeting and Diana must have hoped they were true converts to Mosley's cause. Nancy never liked Mosley himself – 'Sir Ogre' as she called him – and had an instinctive aversion to the violence implicit in his methods, but at first she defended his policies. Indeed there were aspects of the Fascist viewpoint that chimed with her own. Evelyn Waugh reminded her many years later that they had quarrelled after she attended a BUF meeting at the Albert Hall. 'Did we,' Nancy replied, 'I'd quite forgotten. I remember Prod [Peter] looked very pretty in a black shirt. But we were young & high spirited then & didn't know about Buchenwald.' Nancy shared with Fascism the belief that Western civilisation was decaying and in need of change; but while the BUF's millenarian vision was of a bright new Britain, she looked back with nostalgia to a vanished past, where a public-spirited aristocracy still lived on the land and where 'sensible men of ample means' ruled the country – a patrician point of view that threads through much of her writing.

Even when being sincere, Nancy could not take herself seriously. In July 1934 she contributed an article, 'Fascism as I See It', to the *Vanguard*, a journal edited by Alexander Ratcliffe, the anti-Catholic, anti-Semitic founder of the Scottish Protestant League. It is a curious piece of writing, not least because much of it is an only slightly toned-down version of the hymn to Fascism that Eugenia proclaims from an overturned washtub at the beginning of *Wigs on the Green*. It is not clear whether Nancy wrote the article then realised she had the germ of a novel, or whether she had already started *Wigs on the Green* and conveniently lifted Eugenia's speech for the *Vanguard*. Nor is it known why she agreed to contribute to the magazine in the first place; *Vogue* and *The Lady* had been the usual outlets for her journalism until then. The article begins soberly enough by explaining that Fascism was an attitude of mind that could no more be understood by people of the old school than Picasso by admirers of representational art. It goes on, with mounting pomposity, to decry the moral turpitude of an age where 'respect for parents, love of the home, veneration of the marriage tie' was at a discount and where allegiance to 'a great and good Leader' was the one thing that could lift the country 'from the slough of despond in which for too long it has weltered.' It ends on a note of pure bombast – as does Eugenia's peroration – with the description of old politicians creeping about Westminster like withered tortoises, 'warming themselves in the synthetic sunlight of each others' approbation,' before being commanded by the Leader to choose between 'ignominy and a Roman death.'

The article was taken seriously by Edgell Rickword, the Communist founding editor of *Left Review*, who described it in that journal as 'a very well-developed case of leaderolatry'. But Unity was not deceived and realised that Nancy was parodying Mosley at his most messianic. 'I'm furious about it,' she wrote to her, 'You might have a little thought for poor me, all the boys know that you're my sister you know.' In the same letter, she struck a cautioning note about *Wigs on the Green*, 'Now seriously, about that book. I have heard a bit about it from Muv [Lady Redesdale], & I warn you you can't *possibly* publish it, so you'd better not waste any more time on it. Because if you did publish it I couldn't *possibly* ever speak to you again.'

Unity's reaction on reading the novel is not recorded. Shortly after its publication, she admitted to Diana that she had not yet read it but that Nancy had written to assure her that she wouldn't mind it, in fact that she would 'positively *like* it', adding, 'she [Nancy] does have quaint ideas.' Perhaps when Unity eventually came to read the book she found her portrait as a beautiful blonde goddess sufficiently gratifying to take the sting out of Nancy's teases. Certainly the few surviving letters exchanged between the sisters after publication are in the same light-hearted tone as before, with Nancy addressing her sister affectionately as 'Head of Bone and Heart of Stone', and joshing her with a poem in mock German.

When Nancy was writing *Wigs on the Green*, Unity had not yet met Hitler, his policies had not yet resulted in systematic genocide and it was still possible – by turning a blind eye to the nature of the regime – to believe that National Socialism could regenerate Germany and usher in an era of peace in Europe. Unity was an impressionable nineteen-year-old when she accompanied Diana to the 1933 Nuremberg Parteitag and came under the spell of Nazism, and just twenty-five when Britain declared war on Germany. Unable to face a conflict between the two countries she loved, she went to a public garden in Munich and put a pistol to her head. The bullet failed to kill her but left her brain-damaged and she died of meningitis nine years later. During the five years she spent in Germany, Unity came to know Hitler personally and embraced the Nazi creed whole-heartedly, including its most virulent anti-Semitism. Nazism, as she wrote to a cousin, 'is my religion, not merely my political party'.

The dark side of Unity's character is plain enough to see: ruthlessness, naïveté and a love of showing off, combined with an attraction to violence and a desire to shock, produced moral blindness of an extreme kind. More difficult to understand is what so endeared her to those who loved her, which her family and friends did, however much they deplored her politics. The bond between the Mitford sisters was strong but it did not stop Jessica from cutting Diana out of her life when politics drove them apart; yet she never broke off relations with Unity, even though they took opposite political sides. 'So what was lovable about her?' Jessica wrote to Unity's biographer, 'and why did I adore her, which I really did . . . There is a dimension, or facet, of her character missing in your book; but what is it, exactly? . . . Well she was so 'uge and obdgegjoinable,[2] such a joke, after *Wigs on the Green* partly a Nancy-created joke – and she [Unity] saw the joke of herself.' Diana described her as 'intelligent and affectionate' and her funeral as the saddest day of her life. To Deborah, the youngest sister, she was, 'funny and loyal and brave'. Lady Redesdale, who assumed the demanding task of caring for her daughter after her suicide attempt, wrote after her death, 'I shall miss her always, she was a most rare character.'

In *Wigs on the Green*, the riddle that was Unity is seen through her eldest sister's distinctive lens. Nancy paints a caricature of an already larger-than-life young woman, under-educated, overprotected and wilful, who takes up politics to fill the void of boredom that is her life. The adolescent aspects of the Jackshirt movement – belonging to a gang, dressing-up in uniform and devotion to a leader – appeal to her strongly; just as the emotional charge of Fascism did to the youth of the 1930s. 'When you find

[2] 'Huge and objectionable' in Boudledidge, the private language in which Unity and Jessica communicated as children.

schoolgirls like Eugenia going mad about something,' one of the characters declares, 'you can be pretty sure that it is nonsense.' Nancy, like many others at the time, underestimated the lethal consequences of the 'nonsense'.

The novel is Nancy's attempt to make sense of a phenomenon that would ultimately tear Europe and her family apart. When you add to this some vintage Mitfordian jokes and teases (and in Peersmont, the lunatic asylum for batty peers, one of her best conceits) it becomes a very fascinating book indeed. However understandable her objections were to its re-publication three quarters of a century ago, today Nancy's fans and all those curious about a particular slice of twentieth-century history will welcome its return.

Charlotte Mosley, daughter-in-law of Nancy Mitford's sister Diana, is a journalist and editor of several volumes of Mitford family letters.

I

'No, I'm sorry,' said Noel Foster, 'not sufficiently attractive.'

He said this in unusually firm and final accents, and with a determination which for him was rare he hung up his office telephone receiver. He leant back in his chair. 'That's the last time,' he thought. Never again, except possibly in regard to the heiresses he now intended to pursue, would he finish long and dreary conversations with the words, 'Not sufficiently attractive.'

Now that he was leaving the office for good he felt himself in no particular hurry to be off. Unlike other Friday evenings he made no dash for the street; on the contrary he sat still and took a long gloating look round that room which for the last two years had been his prison. With the heavenly knowledge that he would never see them again he was able to gaze in perfect detachment at the stained-glass windows (a cheerful amber shade, full of bubbles too, just like champagne), and the old oak furnishing – which made such a perfectly delightful setting for the charms of Miss Clumps the pretty typist, Miss Brisket the plain typist, and Mr Farmer the head clerk. This amiable trio had been his fellow prisoners for the last two years, he most sincerely hoped never to see any of them again. He said goodbye to them cordially enough, however, took his hat and his umbrella, and then, rich and free, he sauntered into the street.

He had not yet had time since good fortune had befallen him to leave his dreary lodging in Ebury Street, and as a matter of habit returned to it now. He then rang up Jasper Aspect. This he did knowing perfectly well that it was a mistake of the first order. Poor young men who have just received notice of agreeable but moderate legacies can do nothing more stupid than to ring up Jasper Aspect. Noel, who had been intimate with Jasper for most of his life, was aware that he was behaving with deplorable indiscretion, nevertheless some irresistible impulse led him to the telephone where the following conversation took place:

'Hullo Jasper?'

'My dear old boy, I was just going to ring you up myself.'

'Oh, what are you doing to-night?'

'I thought it would be exceedingly agreeable to take a little dinner off you.'

'All right, I wanted to see you; where shall we dine – how about Boulestins? Meet you there at eight?'

'Look here, I haven't got any money, you know.'

'That's all right,' said Noel. He would keep his glorious news until such time as he could see the incredulity and disgust which would no doubt illumine Jasper's honest countenance when it was broken to him. Jasper now once more proclaimed his inability to pay, was once more reassured and rang off.

'This is all exceedingly mysterious,' he said when they met.

'Why?' said Noel.

'Well, my dear old boy, it isn't every day of the week one can get a free meal off you, let alone an expensive one like this is going to be. Why did you choose me for the jolly treat? I find it very puzzling indeed.'

'Oh! I wanted to see you. I want your advice about one or two things actually, and after all one must eat somewhere, so why not here?' And fishing for his handkerchief he produced, as though by accident, and replaced with nonchalance, a roll of ten pound notes.

Jasper's expression did not change however, as Noel had hope-fully anticipated that it would. He merely ordered another champagne cocktail. When it came he said, 'Well, here's to the Scrubs old boy, hope you'll find it comfy there, you can come and see me sometimes in between terms, I'm never at all up-stage about my jail-bird friends.'

'I don't know what you mean,' said Noel, coldly.

'Don't you? Well it's fairly obvious that you've got the skates on, isn't it? And I suppose you want me to help you get away with the dough. Now I suggest that we should go fifty-fifty on it, and do a bunk together. That suit you?'

'No.'

'First of all you had better tell me frankly if you are wanted. I've been wanted in Paris, and not wanted anywhere else, for simply ages, there's nothing I don't know on the subject of wanting.'

'My dear old boy,' said Noel, comfortably. 'I'm afraid you've got hold of the wrong end of the stick.'

'But you came to me for advice.'

'Yes, I did, I thought you might be able to put me in touch with some rich girl who would like to marry me.'

'That's a good one I'm bound to say. To begin with, if I was lucky enough to know any rich girls can you see me handing them out to you? And to go on with, I shouldn't think the girl is born who would like to marry you.'

'Oh! nonsense, girls will marry anybody. Besides, I'm a pretty attractive chap you know.'

'Not very. Anyhow, let me tell you something. Courting heiresses is an exceedingly expensive occupation. You didn't give me time just then to count exactly how much you have managed to extract from the till, but I'm pretty sure it wasn't enough to finance a racket of that sort. Why, you don't know what these girls run you in for, nights out, lunches, orchids, weekends to all parts of the Continent, that's not the beginning, I've been through it, I know what I'm talking about. I suppose the worst part of it,' he went on, warming to his subject, 'is the early-morning telephoning. The precious little poppet, buried in lace pillows, likes to have a nice long cosy chat between 9 and 10 a.m., she doesn't realize that you, meanwhile, are shivering half-way up your landlady's staircase with an old woman scrubbing the linoleum round your feet. And what's the end of it all? When she marries her Roumanian prince she may remember to ask you to be one of those pretty young gentlemen who leave the guests to find their own pews at weddings. It's all fearfully dismal I can tell you.'

'How you do talk,' said Noel admiringly. 'Just like a book. I wonder you don't write one.'

'I shall, when I'm thirty. Nobody ought to write books before they're thirty. I hate precocity. Now then, out with it, Noel, how did you get all that cash?'

'Well, if you really want to know, an aunt of mine has died. She has left me some money.'

'That's just an ordinary lie, of course. Legacies never happen to people one knows. It's like seeing ghosts or winning the Irish Sweep, one never meets the people who have, only people who know people who have. So how much did she leave you?'

'Three thousand three hundred and fourteen pounds.'

'Just say that again.'

'Three thousand three hundred and fourteen pounds.'

'Did I hear you say three thousand three hundred and fourteen pounds?'

'You did.'

'Honest to God?'

'Honest to God.'

'D'you think the aunt was in full possession of her faculties when she made that will?'

'There's no doubt that she was.'

'Such a very odd sum. Well now, Noel, my dear old boy, you have my warmest congratulations. And what about the fourteen pounds?'

'What about them?'

'Hadn't it occurred to you that three thousand three hundred pounds rolls off the tongue much easier without that niggly little fourteen tacked on to it. Sounds more really, I should have said – the fourteen rather spoils it. Actually fourteen pounds is the exact sum I owe my landlady by a curious coincidence.'

'Oh, it is is it?' said Noel in a voice of boredom. 'Now shall I tell you what I said to myself when the lawyer rang me up about all this? I said, no cash presents to any of the boys, and that I keep to, so lay off will you?'

'That was exceedingly sensible of you. So now you intend to devote the whole of this little nest-egg to the pursuit of heiresses?'

'I should very much like to find a nice girl and marry her, if that's what you mean.'

'It's such a fearful gamble. Much better put the money on a horse and be out of your misery at once.'

'I'm not in any misery at all. I intend to lead a soft, luxurious life for the next six months or so, at the rate of six thousand six hundred and twenty-eight pounds a year.'

'And after that a soft uxorious life at an even better rate. I'm bound to say it's quite a pleasing outlook – only you don't know any heiresses.'

'Not at present. I thought perhaps you did.'

'Pass the brandy, old boy.'

'In that case,' said Noel, summoning the waiter. 'I'll have my bill, please – in that case I think I shall have to be going. I've watched you drinking that very expensive brandy for quite long enough.'

'Hold on,' said Jasper in an aggrieved tone of voice, 'give a chap time to think, I've just had an idea – pass the brandy, old boy.' He helped himself, carelessly splashing the brandy into his glass. 'The Jolly Roger,' he said.

'What Jolly Roger?'

'It's a public-house in Chalford where I once stayed when I was shooting the moon. Pretty little place, pretty little barmaid, I remember – Minnie or Winnie or some name like that.'

'Thanks, I know plenty of pretty little barmaids myself. It's not what I'm looking for at present. I think I shall have to be going.'

'Suppose you allow me to finish what I was saying.'

'I beg your pardon.'

'About a mile from Chalford village are the lodge gates of Chalford Park, and there lives the girl whom I believe to be England's largest heiress – Eugenia Malmains. I couldn't make a pass at her then because she was under the age of consent; it was about four years ago. She must be quite seventeen by now though. Nobody knows anything about her because she lives with her grandparents who are batty – she's fairly batty herself I believe.'

'That's nothing. She couldn't be battier than the girls one meets about the place in London. I don't think it sounds worth investigating, but I might go down to the pub for a weekend sometime – where is Chalford?'

'About ten miles away from Rackenbridge, that's the station. Best train in the day is the 4.45 from Paddington.'

'Well, many thanks, old boy. See you before long, I hope.'

'I hope so. Thank you very much for my good dinner.'

They spoke with nonchalance. Neither, however, was the least deceived as to the other's intentions, nor was Noel at all surprised when, arriving at Paddington next day to catch the 11.50 to Rackenbridge, he saw Jasper waiting for him on the platform.

Sadly he lent the requisite pound for Jasper's ticket, drearily he followed him into a first-class luncheon car. Poor young men who have just received notice of agreeable but moderate legacies should know better than to ring up Jasper Aspect.

'I've no one to blame but myself,' thought Noel, gloomily.

2

'Britons, awake! Arise! oh, British lion!' cried Eugenia Malmains in thrilling tones. She stood on an overturned wash-tub on Chalford village green and harangued about a dozen aged yokels. Her straight hair, cut in a fringe, large, pale-blue eyes, dark skin, well-proportioned limbs and classical features, combined with a certain fanaticism of gesture to give her the aspect of a modern Joan of Arc.

She was dressed in an ill-fitting grey woollen skirt, no stockings, a pair of threadbare plimsolls, and a jumper made apparently out of a Union Jack. Round her waist was a leather belt to which there was attached a large bright dagger.

Noel Foster and Jasper Aspect were taking a short walk round the village waiting for 'them' to open. The true amateur of bars, be it noted, is seldom content to drink his beer in his own hotel, where he may have it in comfort at any hour; he is always restlessly awaiting the glorious moment when some other 'they' shall be available. This is called pub-crawling, a sport much indulged in by gentlemen of the leisured classes.

Suddenly they came upon the godlike apparition of Eugenia Malmains on her wash-tub. They gasped.

'That's the girl we want,' said Jasper suddenly, 'that's Eugenia. I didn't recognize her at first. I'm bound to say she's become exceedingly beautiful since I was here, but she's evidently quite batty just like I told you. Still you can't have everything in this life. D'you mind if I make a pass at her too, old boy?'

'Yes I do, you're not to,' said Noel peevishly, 'and anyway shut up. I want to hear what she's saying.'

'The Union Jack Movement is a youth movement,' Eugenia cried passionately, 'we are tired of the old. We see things through

7

their eyes no longer. We see nothing admirable in that debating society of aged and corrupt men called Parliament which muddles our great Empire into wars or treaties, dropping one by one the jewels from its crown, casting away its glorious Colonies, its hitherto undenied supremacy at sea, its prestige abroad, its prosperity at home, and all according to each vacillating whim of some octogenarian statesman's mistress —'

At this point a very old lady came up to the crowd, pushed her way through it and began twitching at Eugenia's skirt. 'Eugenia, my child,' she said brokenly, 'do get off that tub, pray, please get down at once. Oh! when her ladyship hears of this I don't know what will happen.'

'Go away Nanny,' said Eugenia, who in the rising tide of oratory seemed scarcely aware that she had been interrupted. 'How could anyone,' she continued, 'feel loyalty for these ignoble dotards, how can the sacred fire of patriotism glow in any breast for a State which is guided by such apathetic nonentities? Britons, I beseech you to take action. Oh! British lion, shake off the nets that bind you.' Here the old lady again plucked Eugenia's skirt. This time however, Eugenia turned round and roared at her, 'Get out you filthy Pacifist, get out I say, and take your yellow razor gang with you. I will have free speech at my meetings. Now will you go of your own accord or must I tell the Comrades to fling you out? Where are my Union Jackshirts?' Two hobbledehoys also dressed in red, white and blue shirts here came forward, saluted Eugenia and each taking one of the Nanny's hands they led her to a neighbouring bench where she sat rather sadly but unresistingly during the rest of the speech.

'We Union Jackshirts,' remarked Eugenia to the company at large, 'insist upon the right to be heard without interruption at our own meetings. Let the Pacifists' – here she gave her Nanny a very nasty look – 'hold their own meetings, we shall not interfere with them at all, but if they try to break up our meetings they do so at their own risk. Let me see, where had I got to – oh! yes. Patriotism is one of the primitive virtues of mankind. Allow it to atrophy and much that is valuable in human nature must perish. This is being proved today, alas, in our unhappy island as well as in those other countries, which, like ourselves, still languish 'neath the deadening sway of a putrescent democracy. Respect for parents, love of the home, veneration of the marriage tie, are all at a discount in England today, society is rotten with vice, selfishness, and indolence. The rich have betrayed their trust, preferring the fetid atmosphere of cocktail-bars and night-clubs to the sanity of a useful country life. The great houses of England, one of her most envied attributes, stand empty – why? Because the great families of England herd together in luxury flats and spend their patrimony in the divorce courts. The poor are no better than the rich, they also have learnt to put self before State, and satisfied with the bread and circuses which are flung to them by their politicians, they also take no steps to achieve a better spirit in this unhappy land.'

'The girl's a lunatic but she's not stupid,' said Jasper.

'My friends, how can we be saved? Who can lift this country from the slough of Despond in which she has for too long wallowed, to a Utopia such as our corrupt rulers have never pictured, even in their wildest dreams? He who aims highest will reach the highest goal, but how can those ancient dipsomaniacs reach any goal at all? Their fingers are paralysed with gout – they cannot aim; their eyesight is impeded with the film of age – they see no goal. The best that they can hope is that from day to day they may continue to creep about the halls of Westminster like withered tortoises seeking to warm themselves in the synthetic sunlight of each other's approbation.'

'I'm liking this,' said Jasper, 'my father's brother is a M.P.'

'How then, if a real sun shall arise, arise with a heat which will shrivel to cinders all who are not true at heart? How if a real Captain, a man, and not a tortoise, shall appear suddenly at their adulterous bedsides, a cup of castor oil in the one hand, a goblet of hemlock in the other, and offer them the choice between ignominy and a Roman death?

'Britons! That day is indeed at hand. There is a new spirit abroad, a new wine that shall not be poured into those ancient bottles. Britons are at last coming to their senses, the British lion is opening his mouth to roar, the attitude of mind which we call Social Unionism is going to save this country from her shameful apathy. Soon your streets will echo 'neath the tread of the Union Jack Battalions, soon the day of jelly-breasted politicians shall be no more, soon we shall all be living in a glorious Britain under the wise, stern, and beneficent rule of Our Captain.'

'Hooray,' cried Jasper, clapping loudly at this stirring peroration, 'Hear! hear! splendid!' The villagers turned and looked at him in amazement. Eugenia gave him a flashing smile.

'Now, Britons,' she continued, 'do you wish to ask any questions? If so I will devote ten minutes to answering them.'

The yokels stood first on one foot and then on the other. Finally one of them removed a straw from his mouth and remarked that they had all enjoyed Miss Eugenia's speech very much, he was sure, and how was His Lordship's hay-fever?

'Better, thank you,' said Eugenia politely, 'it always goes away in July, you know.' She looked disappointed. 'No more questions? In that case I have an announcement to make. Anyone wishing to join our Union Jack Movement can do so by applying to me, either here or at Chalford House. You are asked to pay ninepence a month, the Union Jack shirt costs five shillings, and the little emblem is sixpence. Would any of you care to join up now?'

The yokels immediately began to fade away. Already they paid two shillings a year to Lady Chalford towards the Conservative funds, and twopence a week for the Nursing Association; they failed, therefore, to see why any more of their hard-earned money should be swallowed up by the Malmains family. Jasper and Noel, on the other hand, snatched at this heaven-sent opportunity to ingratiate themselves with the heiress. They sprang forward and announced in chorus that they were anxious to be recruited. Eugenia's face lit up with a perfectly radiant smile.

'Oh, good,' she said, coming down from her tub. She then began hitching up her skirt, disclosing underneath it a pair of riding breeches, from the pocket of which she produced two recruiting cards and a fountain-pen. 'You sign here – see? You have to promise that you will obey the Captain in all things and pay ninepence.'

'I promise,' said Jasper.

'It's all very well,' said Noel, 'I suppose that's O.K., but look here, who is the Captain? Is he a nice chap? Couldn't I promise to obey him in most things? He might want me to do something very peculiar, mightn't he?'

Eugenia looked at him with lowering brow, fingering her dagger. 'You had better be careful,' she said gloomily. 'That is no way to speak of the Captain.'

'I'm awfully sorry,' said Noel, nervously eyeing the weapon. 'I'll never do it again. Right then, here's my ninepence.'

'Lend me a bob, old boy,' said Jasper.

'Sorry, old boy,' said Noel.

'Don't be a cad, you swine,' said Jasper, kicking him gently on the shin.

'Here, don't kick me,' said Noel.

Eugenia looked from one to the other. Her sympathies were clearly with Jasper. 'Are you perhaps unemployed?' she asked him, 'because if you are it's only fourpence.'

'Am I unemployed? Is unemployed my middle name? Lend me fourpence, old boy.'

'Sorry, old boy.'

'I will lend you fourpence,' said Eugenia suddenly, 'but you will have to pay me back soon, because what I really came down for this afternoon was to buy two twopenny bars at the village shop.'

'Bars of what?'

'Chocolate, of course.'

On hearing this Noel was naturally obliged to produce fourpence for Jasper. Eugenia then persuaded him to pay for both their Union Jack shirts and little emblems as well. He thought that Fate, as usual, was being wonderful to Jasper, who was quite obviously top boy in Eugenia's estimation, and who now capped all by suggesting that they should repair to the village shop in search of twopenny bars. While Noel paid for the bars he realized that the credit for them was going to Jasper. He decided that he must return this old-man-of-the-sea to London as soon as might be.

'I've never seen you before, do you live near here?' Eugenia asked Noel, as they all emerged, munching twopenny bars, from the village shop.

'No, we don't, we are just staying at the Jolly Roger for a few weeks, or at least that is to say I am staying for a few weeks. My friend, Mr Aspect here, has to leave tomorrow, quite early. It is very unfortunate.'

'Don't you believe it,' said Jasper shortly, 'not now I've met you, I'm not leaving. No such thing.'

'Oh! good,' said Eugenia, 'it would really be too sad if you had to go, just when you've joined the Movement and everything. You're the type of young men I need in this village, keen, active, energetic.'

'That's me,' said Jasper.

'Besides, you won't be busy doing other things all day. I have some wonderful members in my detachment, but, of course, they are all working boys, except my two Union Jackshirt defenders you saw just now dealing with that old female Pacifist. I thought they did it very bravely; she would have razored them up for twopence, no tricks are too filthy for that gang, it seems. Yes, what we need here is educated people of leisure like yourselves, for canvassing and platform work. That's why I'm so particularly glad you're staying on.'

'I suppose you are Eugenia Malmains?' said Jasper. 'I used to see you riding about the village here years ago when you were under the age of – quite a kid you know. You lived alone with your grand-parents then.'

'I still do, worse luck.'

'Always down here? Don't you ever go to London?'

'No, you see, T.P.O.F. (that's what I always call my grandmother, it stands for The Poor Old Female) says that nobody would speak to us in London if we did go. T.P.O.M. (The Poor Old Male, that's my grandfather) used to go up to the House of Lords, before he had his stroke. As he was stone deaf it didn't matter so much whether people spoke to him or not. It wouldn't matter to me a bit, either, because I know the comrades at the Union Jack House would speak to me. T.P.O.F. has got a bee in her bonnet about it.'

'Do you want to go?'

'Of course I want to. I should see the Captain if I did, besides, I could march with the Union Jack Battalions.'

'Who is the Captain?'

'Captain Jack, founder of the Social Unionist Movement and Captain of the Union Jackshirts,' said Eugenia, throwing up her hand in a salute.

'Why don't you marry and get away from here?'

'Thank you, I am wedded to the Movement though. Oh! bother, here comes Nanny again, I must go.' She put her hands to her mouth and called, on two peculiar notes, 'Vivian Jack-son.' A small black horse without saddle or bridle came trotting up to her, accompanied by an enormous mastiff. 'This is Vivian Jackson, my horse,' she explained. 'My dog is called the Reichshund, after Bismarck's dog you know. Goodbye.' She swung herself on to the horse's back, gave it a resounding smack on one side of its neck, and galloped away in the direction of Chalford Park.

'Thank God for our English eccentrics,' said Jasper. 'Come on, old boy, they must be open by now.'

3

'What's the news?' asked Noel. He came into the garden of the Jolly Roger feeling hot and grumpy after a long walk. Noel, when in the country, always took large doses of fresh air and exercise. He believed in looking after his health. Jasper, who believed in having a good time, sat smoking cigarettes and reading the morning papers, which, it seemed, could be expected to arrive in that remote village, together with the one post, at any hour between 10 a.m. and 4 p.m.

'Another body has been found in another trunk and two fearfully pretty Janes turned up here late last night. It appears that they intend to stay several days – just what we needed.'

'I don't see why,' said Noel petulantly. 'We've got Eugenia.'

'Don't you just? Well it's like this old boy, the more the merrier. You can't have enough of a good thing. Many hands make light work. And so on. Rather nice about the body too, the one in the trunk I mean. In fact I'm very suited by this place altogether.'

'Are you?'

'I am. I also had three minutes' conversation with Eugenia before Nanny got at us. Enchanting girl, I quite expect I shall marry her.'

'Jasper, old boy, there's something I must say to you. It's not very easy for me, but I've known you long enough, I hope, to be able to speak my mind to you.'

'That's quite all right, old boy, don't you worry. I've got some money coming in any day now – I shan't be touching you for another penny I promise you.'

Noel sighed deeply. He might have foreseen that this old-man-of-the-sea would be hard to shake off.

'So what had Eugenia to say for herself?' he asked with some irritation.

'A lot more about how we are governed by octogenarian states-men's mistresses. I'm bound to say it's a shaking thought, isn't it?'

'Which are octogenarians, the statesmen or their mistresses?'

'Oh, I see. I must remember to ask her that some time. Which-ever it is they must certainly be got rid of. Ignominy or a Roman death for them. Good – here's the beer at last – some for you, old boy? Two more beers please miss, and put all that down to room 6, will you?'

'Room 8,' said Noel. His room was 6.

'Oh, dear, now you're going to be mean,' said Jasper. 'Put two down to room 6 and one down to room 8, and put the newspapers down to room 6 – no good old boy, you'll have to read about the trunk sooner or later you know. I must say I hate all this cheese-paring.'

'So do I,' said Noel eagerly. 'Tell you what, Jasper, I'll give you this for your fare back to London and pay your bill here when you've gone. How's that?'

'Exceedingly generous of you,' said Jasper, tucking thirty shil-lings into his note-case and settling down to more grisly details of the trunk murders.

Later that day he remarked to Noel; 'I say, there's something very queer indeed about those new Janes. First of all they've signed the book here as Miss Smith and Miss Jones, both of Rickmans-worth. Likely tale. Then they've taken a private sitting-room, which strikes me as odd. But the oddest thing of all is that the Miss Jones one spent her whole afternoon in the orchard picking ducal coro-nets out of her drawers and nightdresses. Bit fishy, the whole business I'm thinking.'

'How d'you know they were ducal coronets?'

'My dear old boy, I know a ducal coronet when I see it. You forget that my grandfather is a duke.'

'Not a proper one.'

'I imagine that proper is just what he isn't anything else but. Not much chance for impropriety when one has been binned-up for thirty-five years, eh?'

'That's just it. I don't count dukes that are binned-up same way I don't count bankrupt dukes.'

'Well, I mean, count him or not as you like. I'm sure he doesn't mind.'

'Go on telling me about Miss Jones's drawers, won't you?'

'As soon as I made quite sure she was picking some kind of monogram out of them (I couldn't see as well as I should have liked, through the hedge) I legged it upstairs to her bedroom, number 4, opposite the bath, and it's full of ducal coronets wherever you look. On the brushes and combs even, the whole place is a regular riot of strawberry leaves. And the jewels she's got lying about on her dressing-table! I managed to find two quid in cash as well, in the pocket of an old mackintosh – shouldn't think she'll miss it.'

'You must be quite nicely off for cash now.'

'Mm. But isn't it extraordinary about Miss Jones. Is she an absconding duchess or a duchess's absconding ladies' maid or what? Anyway, I'll stand you a drink at the Rose Revived. Eugenia should be round before long and I promised we'd meet her outside the twopenny-bar shop.'

Eugenia, however, was in the middle of a gruelling interview with The Poor Old Female, her grandmother, who had come to hear something of her recent activities.

'My child I cannot have you running round the village like a kitchen-maid,' T.P.O.F. was saying, sadly rather than angrily, 'talking to strangers, worse than that, accepting sweets from them. Besides, I hear that you have been riding that pony of yours astride again – you are not a baby any more, my dear, and young ladies should not ride in that way. What must the village people think of you? I blame nurse for all this and I blame myself; I suppose I can hardly blame you, Eugenia. After all, your mother was a wicked sinful woman, and bad blood always comes out sooner or later.'

'I'm not bad at all,' said Eugenia, sullenly. 'I never do sins, and I would gladly lay down my life for the Captain.'

Lady Chalford, who vaguely supposed that Eugenia must be

referring to the Deity, looked embarrassed. Religious fervour was, in her eyes, almost as shocking as sexual abandon, and quite likely to be associated with it. Many of the most depraved women whom she had known in her social days, had been deeply and ostentatiously religious.

She went to church herself, of course, feeling it a patriotic duty so to do, but she had no personal feelings towards God, whom she regarded as being, conjointly with the King, head of the Church of England. However, if the girl was really obsessed by religion, a tendency which Lady Chalford had never noticed in her before, and which she presumed to be of recent origin, it might yet be possible to save her from following in her mother's steps. Lady Chalford considered whether or not it would be advisable to call in the parson. Meanwhile she forced herself to say rather shyly, 'The Captain was always obedient to those in authority. Try to follow His example, Eugenia.'

'I don't agree at all,' was the reply. 'The Captain's ideas are most revolutionary, most, and he doesn't have to obey anyone, being a Leader.'

Lady Chalford knew herself to be unfitted for a theological argument on these lines. She decided that the parson would have to be called in.

'Give unto Caesar the things that are Caesar's,' she said vaguely. 'I suppose if you follow Him you won't come to much harm. But pray don't let me hear of you careering about the village and speaking to strange men, or you will end as your mother did.'

'How did she?' asked Eugenia, with passionate interest. Lady Chalford refused to be trapped in this manner. It was not a subject which she considered suitable for discussion, still less suitable for the ears of a young lady whom it concerned so intimately. The ugly word 'divorce' would have to be spoken, even uglier words understood. Sooner or later, of course, Eugenia must be informed, but the news would surely come best from the child's own husband, if Fate were sufficiently kind to provide her with one. Lady Chalford was haunted by sad forebodings on this subject, no nice man, she felt sure, would wish to marry the daughter of Eugenia's mother; different propositions were more likely to be made.

'Go to your room now until dinner-time. I am extremely vexed with you.'

'Stupid old female,' Eugenia muttered under her breath. She obeyed, however. Indeed, until the Social Unionists had come to fill the void of boredom that was her life, she had always obeyed her grandparents in everything. It had never occurred to her to do otherwise.

So Jasper and Noel awaited her in vain outside the twopenny-bar shop. They were not, however, left without any distraction. Hardly had they taken up a position on Ye Olde Stocks (which had been placed on the village green by some enthusiastic lover of the countryside in about 1890, and had since constituted a lure for Americans) than the Misses Smith and Jones appeared in search of aspirins, soap, and a daily paper. The first two were procurable, the last was not. Miss Smith and Miss Jones emerged from the village shop loudly bewailing this fact. Jasper saw and took his opportunity.

'Do let me lend you my *Daily Mail*,' he said, addressing himself to the ducal Miss Jones while comprising in his glance the rather more luscious-looking Miss Smith.

'Oh, thank you, that is very kind,' said Miss Smith. Miss Jones almost snatched at the paper. She then began to race through its pages while Miss Smith looked eagerly over her shoulder. They seemed to be searching for some particular piece of news.

'Second body in trunk is on the middle page,' said Jasper quietly. 'The missing ladies are on page 8.'

Horror appeared on the faces of Miss Smith and Miss Jones. 'What missing ladies?' asked Miss Smith in a shaking voice.

'The ones the police suspect of being in more trunks,' said Jasper, looking at them with a thoughtful expression. They appeared very much relieved by this. 'Will you have a cigarette?'

Miss Smith took one. Miss Jones did not smoke. They continued, in a desultory way, to examine the paper, but apparently failing to find anything of interest in it they gave it back to Jasper.

'As we all appear to be using the same bathroom and so on, and so forth,' he said, 'supposing we introduce ourselves. I am Jasper Aspect and this is Noel Foster, who is down here in order to have a complete rest. He has been far from well lately, thoroughly run down.'

Noel gave Jasper a look which, if looks could kill, would have killed him. Too late, the harm was now done. Of no avail to expostulate or deny, the impression had duly been made and registered of a boring hypochondriac. Once more he cursed himself for letting Jasper join in this adventure. Alone he could have stood up to each situation as it arose, cutting quite a romantic figure. Jasper was always just too quick for him. He ground his teeth and thought of vengeance, after all his was the upper hand financially.

It appeared that Miss Smith was called Poppy. She seemed to like Jasper and expressed sympathy for Noel, whose appearance probably failed to attract her. Miss Jones did not vouchsafe her name, neither did she join in the conversation which followed, but stood tapping long white fingers on her bag, as though anxious to get away.

Miss Smith asked how long Jasper was stopping at the Jolly Roger.

'I expect we shall be here for some weeks. I am engaged upon research work in the neighbourhood, of a delicate and interesting nature, and Noel has his cure. He has had a very sad time lately – the aunt with whom he lived died suddenly.'

Miss Smith regretted. Noel raged inwardly. From now onwards he was stamped as a delicate young man who had always lived with his aunt, a woman whom actually he had seen about four times in his life.

'And you,' continued Jasper, 'how long shall you be here?'

It appeared that Miss Smith felt herself suited by Chalford, but that Miss Jones did not. 'My friend,' said Miss Smith, rather nervously, 'er – Miss Jones here, finds the Jolly Roger so very uncomfortable. The bath isn't built in, as you have probably noticed, and she is not used to sharing a bathroom with other people. The beds, too, are rather hard.'

'I didn't know that Rickmansworth was noted for its sybarites,' said Jasper.

'Rickmansworth?' said Miss Smith vaguely – then pulling herself together, 'Oh, Rickmansworth you mean? Where we come from? Is a liking for the ordinary comforts of life limited within geographic boundaries? I never heard it.'

'The Jolly Roger is fitted with more than the ordinary comforts of life. The place is clean, the food eatable, the beer extraordinarily good, while as for the bath it is often quite nice and warm you know, and now that, as I see, you have bought some soap, we shall all be able to have a good wash in it.'

Miss Jones shuddered. Opening her mouth for the first time she remarked in a sort of high wail that she was going to grease her face and lie down for a bit. She then walked quickly away. Jasper noticed, on the fourth finger of Miss Smith's left hand, a palpable wedding-ring of small diamonds. He was not displeased, and suggested that they should take a stroll together.

It was now that Noel, wandering gloomily by himself, ran into Mrs Lace, the Local Beauty.

4

Every country neighbourhood has its local beauty, and Chalford provided no exception to this rule. Anne-Marie Lace, however, was not quite the usual type of faded fluffy little woman whose large blue eyes attract a yearly-diminishing troop of admirers at the covert side or on the tennis court. She was lacking in any sporting accomplishments; she was intellectually pretentious; she was ambitious, and she was really beautiful. It was her tragedy that she was born, bred and married in the country.

In London, with her looks and energetic will to please, she could undoubtedly have made an entrance into that sort of society which she longed for, the semi-intellectual society which is much photographed and often spoken of in the newspapers. Even in the vicinity of Chalford, wretchedly narrow as was the field it had to offer, she was something of a star, and indeed was known to the gentry for many miles around as 'the beautiful Mrs Lace'. She had the satisfaction of knowing that most of the women disliked her, while their husbands, loutish boors whom she despised, thought her lovely but much too highbrow. This was satisfactory, still more so was the whole-hearted adulation which was laid at her feet by some ten or twelve rather weedy youths, who formed every summer a kind of artistic colony in thatched cottages near Rackenbridge. They supposed her to be rich, ate quantities of free meals beneath her roof, and painted incompetent little pictures of her in the most extravagant poses. They also helped to design her clothes which were always an endless topic of local conversation as she never could resist appearing at everyday functions in elaborate fancy dress. The black velvet, fur hat and ear-rings of a Russian Grand Duchess, the livid greens and yellows of a Bakst ballet dancer, taffeta bustle and Alexandra fringe, Mandarin tunic and trousers, making each its appearance on some most inappropriate occasion aroused each in turn, among tweeded local ladies, a storm of discussion and criticism, the repercussions of which reached Mrs Lace, by no means displeasing her.

Nevertheless Mrs Lace was a thoroughly discontented woman, neither her house, her husband nor her children afforded her any satisfaction. The house, Comberry Manor, had belonged to the parents of Major Lace and was very nondescript. In vain did she beg that she might redecorate it to her own taste, thus giving expression to the aesthetic side of her nature by painting every wall white and having all the furniture pickled.

Major Lace refused to spend a penny in that direction; he liked his house very well as it was, so poor Mrs Lace was obliged to confine her activities to the bathroom, which she papered entirely with pictures out of *Vogue*, curtaining it with oilcloth. This she did with her own hands, under the supervision of an artistic young man from Rackenbridge called Mr Leader.

Her husband was considered by Anne-Marie and her satellites to be a terrible drag upon his exquisite wife. In fact, he was a nice, simple, ordinary man, with few ideas beyond the suitable mating of his prize Jersey cows. He was no longer in love with Anne-Marie, but still took her at her own valuation, was proud of her beauty, and considered that she was the very glass of fashion and the mould of form. This did not, however, ensure him making the requisite allowances for her artistic temperament, often he irritated her profoundly when she was in one of her moods, by saying, 'Don't be ratty, old girl,' and stumping off to his cowsheds. She would long on such occasions to pay him back with secret infidelities, but the Rackenbridge young men, whilst only too ready to profess undying love for her, were idle fellows and never seemed to contemplate adultery.

As a result, little Caroline and little Romola both had tow-coloured hair, moon-shaped faces, and pale-blue eyes like the Major, and were, like him, stolid unimaginative personalities. They were a great disappointment to their mother.

As soon as Mrs Lace heard, by means of Major Lace's old governess who lived in one of his cottages and was a great gossip, that four people, all of them quite young, had come to stay at the Jolly Roger, she nipped round to have a look at the visitors' book. The Jolly Roger was in many ways rather superior to the ordinary village inn, it had a reputation for good English cooking, cleanliness, and an adequate cellar, and was for this reason visited every now and then by quite notable people. Authors, actors, antiquarians, and distinguished members of various professions came there, and their names were treasured by Mr Birk, the landlord, but although Anne-Marie always kept an eye on the book, she found that the guests were usually too old, or their visits too short for them to be of much use to her. Today the signatures seemed more promising. It is true that she had never heard either of Noel Foster or of the Rickmansworth sybarites; on the other hand Jasper Aspect's name was a name with which she was acquainted. She instantly planned to go home and change her clothes which were at present of the Paris-Plage variety. Mr Aspect, a well-known figure in society circles, was probably tired of sophistication and would be more likely to take an interest in simplicity and rural charm. Her Austrian-Tyrolean peasant's dress would meet the case exactly. Delighted with the subtlety of this reasoning she hurried away in the direction of Comberry. On the village green, however, she met Noel, decided to waste no time, and weighed-in with an old conversational gambit.

'Excuse me,' she said, 'have you seen two rather sweet children in a donkey-cart?'

Noel had not. This was to have been expected, considering that, as Mrs Lace very well knew, the said children were at home playing in the garden, where they had been all day.

'Oh! the monkeys,' she continued playfully, 'you can't imagine how frightening it is to have a family. They do most awfully unnerving things. Where in the world can *les petites méchancetés* have got to now?'

And she flapped her eyelids at Noel, who remarked, as indeed he was meant to, that she did not look old enough to have a family.

23

'Me? I'm terribly old. Actually I was married more or less out of the nursery.' She sighed, and opening her eyes to their full extent she looked at the ground. Poor kid, poor exquisite little creature, trapped into the drudgery of marriage before she knew anything about life and love. Noel's most chivalrous instincts were aroused, he thought her extremely beautiful, far more to his taste than Miss Smith, Miss Jones, or Eugenia. He felt thankful that, for once, Jasper was nowhere about.

'Who are you?' asked Mrs Lace prettily. 'Perhaps you were dropped by magic on to our village green. Anyway, I hope you won't vanish again into a little puff of smoke. *Espérons que non*. Promise you won't do that.'

Noel promised. He then went back with her to Comberry Manor, where he was given cowslip wine, and told a very great deal about Mrs Lace.

She was happily married, she said, to a handsome man called Hubert Lace, who was an old darling, but fearfully jealous, selfish, greedy, and mean. These unpleasant words were not named, but served up with a frothing sauce of sugary chatter. As the old darling was also slightly half-witted he could naturally have no sympathy for Anne-Marie's artistic leanings, and she was therefore obliged to wrap herself up in her garden, her children, and the consolations of the intellect. Noel assumed from the fact that her name, as she told him, was Anne-Marie, from the slightly foreign accent and curious idiom in which she spoke, and from her general appearance, that she was not altogether English. He was wrong, however.

For the first twenty years of her life she had lived in a country vicarage and been called Bella Drage. Being an imaginative and enterprising girl she had persuaded her father to send her to Paris for a course of singing lessons. He scraped together enough money for her to have six months there, after which she came back Anne-Marie by name and Anne-Marie by nature. Shortly after this metamorphosis had occurred she met Hubert Lace, who was enslaved at the Hunt Ball by her flowing dress, Edwardian coiffure and sudden, if inaccurate, excursions into the French language. He laid heart and fortune at her feet. Bella Drage was shrewd enough to realize that she was unlikely to do better for herself, not sufficiently shrewd to foresee an unexpected vein of obstinacy in the Major which was to make him perfectly firm in his refusal to live anywhere but at Comberry. She now knew that her ambition of entertaining smart Bohemians in London could never be realized while she was still married to him. It was one of her favourite day-dreams to envisage the death of Hubert, gored perhaps by a Jersey bull or chawed up by one of those middle-white pigs, who, their energies having been directed by a fad of the Major's towards fields of cabbages rather than the more customary trough, were apt to behave at times with a fearful madness of demeanour. After the funeral and a decent period of mourning, an interesting young widow would then take London by storm. The idea of divorce never occurred to her as an alternative to the demise of poor Hubert. Early up-bringing in the parsonage had not been without its influence upon her and Mrs Lace was at heart a respectable little person.

None of these truths made themselves apparent to Noel. He beheld, as he was meant to behold, a vivid vital creature living in unsuitable surroundings, a humming bird in a rusty cage, a gardenia in a miry bog, a Mariana of the Moated Grange. Eugenia faded into unreality, Miss Smith and Miss Jones might never have been born for all he cared. Jasper could now retire into his proper place as a penniless sycophant, Noel had at last gone one better than him, and found by his own unaided efforts a pearl among women.

They talked and talked over the cowslip wine and Noel began to realize that his pearl was as cultivated as she was beautiful. She was a student of obscure Restoration poetry and early French ballads, so she told him, knew Proust by heart (expressing a pained surprise when he owned that he had only read *Swann's Way*, and that in English), also D. H. Lawrence, Strindberg, Ibsen, which last two she preferred to read in French.

In painting, her taste, it appeared, was catholic. Primitives, Dutch and Italian Renaissance, the English School, French impressionists,

Surréalistes, all was grist that came to her mill; in music her exquisite sensibilities were apparent. She only cared for Bach, Brahms, and Beethoven. Wagner was to her a mere ugly noise, Chopin a sentimental tinkle. She told him that she was born out of her proper time, she could only have been contented in the eighteenth century – this boisterous age, these machine-made nineteen-thirties said nothing to her, she found herself bored, bewildered, and unhappy.

Noel was enchanted. Never before, he thought, had he met a beautiful woman who was at the same time a natural aesthete. He drank a great quantity of cowslip wine and went back to the Jolly Roger, feeling rather sick, but apart from that, tremendously elated.

He joined Jasper in the dining-room. Dinner, Mr Birk told him reproachfully, had been ready for some time. Jasper handed him a note which had just arrived from Eugenia, it was addressed to Union Jackshirt Aspect and Union Jackshirt Foster.

'Hail! The filthy old female Pacifist my grandmother has shut me up in my room because I was seen talking to you. She misuses me and tramples upon me as for many years France has misused and trampled upon Germany. It does not signify. Germany has now arisen and I shall soon arise and my day shall dawn blood red. Terrible must be the fate of the enemies of Social Unionism, so let the poor old female beware. I will meet you both tomorrow outside the twopenny-bar shop at four o'clock exactly.

'Yours in
'Social Unionism,
'EUGENIA MALMAINS.'

This document was adorned with a Swastika, Union Jack, and Skull and Cross-bones, all carefully drawn in black ink.

'She's a fine girl,' said Jasper, with his mouth full. 'I hope to marry her yet. Tell you what, Noel old boy, I'm in love.'

Noel was profoundly irritated by this statement, which took all the wind out of his own sails.

'So am I,' he said.

'Good egg,' said Jasper. They both went on eating in silence for a bit.

'My Miss Smith,' said Jasper, 'is a dangerous good armful. She wriggles in an exceedingly delicious way when you kiss her. I'm fearfully in love.'

Noel thought that there was no point in mentioning that he had not so far kissed his beloved. He wondered now why on earth this was, and supposed that the girl, while perfect in other ways, must be lacking in initiative. 'My girl is called Anne-Marie,' he said, 'Anne-Marie Lace, she is wonderful.'

'How did you pick her up?' asked Jasper with interest.

'We met,' said Noel haughtily, 'on the village green; she was looking for her children.'

'And does she wriggle when you kiss her?'

'Not exactly. She is a most fascinating creature, a natural high-brow. We had a long discussion on art and literature.'

'Sounds a cracking old bore,' said Jasper, 'if there's one thing I can't abide it is culture in women. Miss Smith reads the *Strand Magazine* and hates foreigners. That's all I found out about her intellect, but there's nothing I can't tell you about her physiological reactions. Darling Miss Smith, I love her like hell, Oh, gee – do I love Miss Smith.'

Noel felt jealous. It began to look as though Jasper loved Miss Smith more than he, Noel, loved Mrs Lace. This was extremely boring for Noel, and he wished more than ever that Jasper was back in London.

'You wait until you see Anne-Marie,' he said crossly. 'I should think she'll make that Miss Smith of yours look like a – like a – well, like a twopenny bar.'

'That's right,' said Jasper, 'Miss Smith looks to me like a twopenny bar looks to Eugenia, and I'm sure you can't say fairer than that.'

'What strikes one most particularly about Anne-Marie is her wonderfully original appearance. Her beauty is something different from what we are used to. I suppose it is that she belongs to her environment so exquisitely, she borrows nothing from your smart London women.'

'Yes, I see, a great hulking dairymaid with apple cheeks. Not my type at all, I'm bound to say.'

'Oh! far from that,' said Noel, with a superior smile, 'if anything you would call her exotic. Very pale and delicate looking, with a rare quality that hardly seems to belong to our generation. A *Dame aux Camélias*, if you like.'

'Tubercular is she?' said Jasper. 'You be careful, old boy.'

5

Next day the mystery of Miss Jones's strawberry leaves was solved. Jasper brought the morning papers into Noel's bedroom just before luncheon-time and showed him with glee the large photographs of Miss Jones which appeared in of all them under such headings as 'It should have been her Wedding day', 'Orangeade instead of Orange Blossom' or 'Earl's fatherless daughter's misfortune'. The captions underneath announced, with hysteria, or with dignity, according to the calibre of the newspaper, that Lady Marjorie Merrith, whose marriage to the Duke of Dartford was to have taken place that very day, had been obliged to postpone it indefinitely, as she had been stricken with an attack of scarlet-fever and would therefore be in quarantine for the next six weeks; she was doing as well as could be expected. Lady Marjorie, they went on to say, was the daughter of the Countess of Fitzpuglington and of the late Earl, whose tragic death in the *Titanic* disaster left his wife a widow ere she was a mother, and his only child an orphan at birth.

'She looks all right, considering,' said Noel. He felt even more stupid than usual, having sat up with Jasper until five o'clock that morning talking about love.

'Considering what?'

'Considering she has scarlet-fever.'

'Scarlet-fever my bottom. Try and pull yourself together old boy. How can I help you if you won't help yourself at all? Could you listen to me intelligently for a few minutes, all this is really most interesting from our point of view. You see what has obviously happened – either she can't take the Duke or the Duke can't take her (doesn't matter which) so they decided, or she decided off her own bat, that the only way to break it off at the eleventh hour would be for her to have some illness with a long quarantine.

Good. The interesting part from our point of view is this – next, possibly, to Eugenia Malmains, Lady Marjorie Merrith (Miss Jones) is the greatest heiress in England. I believe it's something fabulous how rich she is. Now here are we, two old bums, with two enormous fortunes dangling in front of our noses. Ours for the asking and God knows we need 'em.'

'What makes you suppose they are ours for the asking?'

'In the case of Eugenia I should have thought it was obvious. She would marry anybody to get away from T.P.O.F. In the case of Lady M. we have a powerful ally in the Rebound. Fantastic what a girl will do on the Rebound. But what I want you to understand now is that we must sketch out a plan of action – it's no good both going for both, that would only end in neither getting either. So we must choose which we want. Now I thought of giving you first choice on condition that you go on financing this racket.'

'I absolutely refuse to lend you another penny, if that's what you're driving at.'

Jasper sighed. 'If you don't,' he said, reluctantly, 'I shall be forced to stay on here insolvent, which would be awkward for you under the circumstances, and make a pass at Mrs Lace.'

Noel saw the force of this argument. Jasper had, before now, broken up many a happy love-affair. 'As a matter of fact old boy,' he said, in a conciliatory tone of voice, 'I was only joking. I like to have you here, it would be awfully dull all alone.'

'Thanks,' said Jasper, 'just choose your girl then will you? I'm rather anxious to get on with the work in hand.'

'My head aches,' said Noel. 'Let me go to sleep again please.'

'You can, as soon as you've chosen. Now, think well, I can't have you changing your mind about this later. Eugenia is richer, more beautiful and madder, Miss Jones is better dressed, more presentable and I should say on the whole lousier. Which will you have?'

'You don't seem to remember that I'm in love already,' said Noel with simple dignity.

'Oh, cut it out. I'm fearfully in love myself. Do you suppose I am going to let that stand in my way? Not likely. There are times, my dear old boy, when love has got to take its proper place as an unethical and anti-social emotion, and this is one of them. Come on, now choose?'

'I will have Eugenia,' Noel muttered into his bed-clothes, 'anything for a quiet life.'

'A quiet life is the last thing you are likely to enjoy with that girl, still have it your own way of course. I shall now go and tee myself up "*très snob pour le sport*" and pursue the elusive Lady Marjorie. I wonder if she's about yet – never knew a girl to be so bedridden, goes to bed early, gets up late, and lies down most of the day with her face greased.'

Noel called out after him that he did not want any luncheon, and once more composed himself for sleep.

Ten minutes later Jasper, contrary to all his plans, was kissing Miss Smith at the bottom of the garden.

'Darling Miss Smith,' he said, 'do you know that I'm madly in love with you?'

'Darling Mr Aspect, are you really? I call that sweet of you.'

'Darling Miss Smith, could one be told who you are?'

'Why do you want to know?'

'Because it happens to interest me.'

'Well, I'm a lot of different things. At the present time I seem to be just a confidante.'

'To Lady Marjorie?'

'Oh! you know that now, do you? Yes, I'm her confidante. When Marge goes mad in white satin with flowers in her hair, I go mad in white linen with straws in my hair (literary allusion), that's what we're up to at the present moment.'

'Yes, I suppose so. Who is your husband?'

'He's called Anthony St Julien, I'm called Poppy St Julien. Call me Poppy if you want to.'

'Thanks, you're Miss Smith to me though. Where is Anthony St Julien now?'

'Having a cocktail somewhere before lunch I should guess.'

'Does he know that Poppy St Julien has been kissing Jasper Aspect under a willow tree, so early in the morning?'

'He does not. Nor, if he did, would he care,' said Mrs St Julien.

'Good heavens, is the man an eel? Now tell me all about the heroine.'

'She's just a heroine you know.'

'In what way so heroic?'

'I mean, she's not ordinary like you and me. One must either regard her as a monstrosity of selfishness or else as a heroine. To me she's a heroine. Her gloves are always so much cleaner than anybody else's, an attribute which I admire.'

'Yes, I see. So why didn't she marry the Duke?'

'You never can tell with Marge why she does this, that or the other. Her mind doesn't work in any comprehensible channels. She just decided to chuck the whole thing the day before yesterday, and then we came down here.'

'Some people don't know when they're lucky,' said Jasper.

'That's what I told her. Marge, I said, in three days' time from now, if you take my advice, you'll be a duch. It's not necessary to look upon that as an end in itself, but think what a useful stepping-stone to all the things one would really like to be – a double duch, for instance, awfully *chic*, you can't be a double duch without being an ordinary one first can you? Then think how enjoyable to be a dowager duch, or even a divorced duch.'

'Or even a dear old duch,' said Jasper.

'But it was all no good, she hardly even listened to me. It appears that romance is what she's after now, or some such nonsense – the girl's been reading trash I suppose. So she left the classical notes on her pincushion, one for Osborne Dartford and one for her mamma, and she fondly imagines that they won't find out where we are hiding, so you won't tell anyone who would matter will you?'

'I won't.'

'And don't let anyone see that we are – well – you know —'

'Walking out you mean?'

'Mm.'

'Why not?'

'Because Anthony St Julien might get to hear of it.'

'I thought you said he wouldn't mind?'

'He wouldn't mind at all, quite the contrary, he'd be pleased. He wants to divorce me on account of he dotes on a débutante.'

'Boy must be batty,' said Jasper. 'If I had a lovely wife like you I'd never go near débutantes.'

'I say, you are sweet.'

'I'm not sweet at all, only sane. So you don't like the idea of being divorced by Anthony St Julien?'

'Of course I don't, why should I? It's most unusual for ladies to be divorced you know, and besides I shouldn't have any money to live on.'

'Why doesn't Anthony Dirty Sweep St Julien let you divorce him?'

'Because it appears that débutantes don't like marrying divorced gentlemen. You see, she won't be a co-respondent herself, and she won't let him take a lady to Brighton either.'

'Sounds like a whist drive,' said Jasper. 'Winning lady moves up, and the losing gentleman moves down. I think your husband is a cad, Miss Smith, if there's one sort of chap I do hate it's a cad.'

'Thank you,' said Poppy St Julien, 'you are really sweet.'

'Sweet's my middle name. Good morning Miss Jones, how did you sleep?'

'Wretchedly, thank you,' said Lady Marjorie, 'You should feel my bed.'

'Oh! I say, I'd like to later on. You know, you must be a real princess, old girl.'

'Are we on old girl terms?'

'Perhaps you're right,' said Jasper. 'By the way, there's a whole heap about you in the papers this morning, orangeade instead of orange blossom. Have you seen it?'

'Yes thanks, I have.'

'I don't think I quite approve of all this careless casting away of dukes you know, dear.'

'Thank you so much. It's immaterial to me what you think about my private affairs. And pray don't call me "dear".'

There was a short silence. Jasper would have liked to get down in good earnest to his conquest of Miss Jones, but felt himself most unaccountably hampered by the presence of Miss Smith. He was very much disgusted by this weakness, and feared that it might indicate the presence of a real emotion.

'Where's your friend?' asked Mrs St Julien.

'Noel? He's doing badly. He's gone and fallen in love with a local beauty, poor old boy.'

'Talking about local beauties,' said Mrs St Julien, 'I've got a mysterious cousin who must live somewhere in this neighbourhood. She's called Eugenia Malmains and nobody has ever clapped eyes on her as far as I know – I thought I'd try and see her while I'm down here.'

'Nothing easier,' said Jasper. 'If you will be outside the twopenny-bar shop this afternoon at four o'clock exactly, I will introduce to you your cousin Eugenia Malmains.'

The day was very hot and breathless. Jasper, Noel, and the two ladies sat beneath a large lime tree on the village green and found little to say to each other. Jasper, who had a great many subjects in common with Mrs St Julien, when alone with her, and who could, he felt sure, have made a most pleasing impression on Lady Marjorie under the same circumstance, found it strangely difficult to deal with the two of them together. The presence of Noel, too, rather cramped his style. Lady Marjorie and Mrs St Julien made desultory conversation, while Jasper bided his time, and Noel silently considered where, when, and how, he should make a declaration to Mrs Lace.

At four o'clock, exactly, Eugenia arrived, swinging down the village street with the gait of a triumphant goddess, and closely followed by Vivian Jackson and the Reichshund. 'Hail!' she cried, throwing up her arm in the Social Unionist salute.

'Snow,' replied Noel, laughing immoderately at this very poor joke.

Eugenia regarded him with lowering brow. 'Union Jackshirt Foster,' she said sternly, 'beware, I have had to speak to you once before. If you continue to be facetious at the expense of our Movement I shall be obliged to degrade you before the comrades. In fact I will cut off all your buttons with my own dagger.'

'Quite right,' said Jasper 'Ignominy or a Roman death for Union Jackshirt Foster. Miss Eugenia, I want to introduce you to your cousin Mrs St Julien, and to Lady Marjorie Merrith. They are staying at the Jolly Roger like us.'

'Hail!' said Eugenia. She saluted each in turn and then shook hands. 'I am very pleased to see you here. We are badly in need of members for a women's branch in this village, perhaps you would help me to organize one?'

'Of course we will,' said Poppy. She was attracted by her cousin.

'Union Jackshirt Aspect,' Eugenia went on, 'I have brought you a message from T.P.O.F. She says that your poor grandfather was one of her greatest friends and she wishes to meet you. Would it be convenient for you to take tea at Chalford House today?'

'Perfectly convenient,' said Jasper. 'I accept with pleasure.'

'Perhaps my cousin would care to come?'

'Thank you, I should like to,' said Poppy St Julien.

Eugenia then rather half-heartedly invited the others. She evidently hoped that they would refuse, which they did. Noel had arranged to visit Mrs Lace at tea-time; Lady Marjorie said that she must grease her face and lie down for a bit.

So the three of them set forth, with Vivian Jackson and the Reichshund trotting at their heels.

'Is it far?' asked Mrs St Julien.

'Oh! no,' Eugenia replied. Her cousin was not much reassured. Eugenia walked with effortless strides, giving the impression that twenty miles to her would be the merest stroll. Quite soon, however, they came upon the lodge gates of Chalford Park, which were large and beautiful, and surmounted by a marble arch of baroque design. The two lodges, one on each side, were small round temples. Inside the park there was an atmosphere of unreality. They advanced up an avenue of elm trees which hung in the sleepy air like large green balloons. The surface of the drive, although in perfect repair, was faintly tinged with mossy green; it was evident that wheeled traffic seldom passed that way.

'Are we approaching the palace of the Sleeping Beauty?' Jasper murmured.

'You will see the house from the top of this rise,' said Eugenia. She looked a little anxious, as though hoping so much that they would like it. She need not have worried. The house, when it appeared to view, presented the most beautiful vision that could be imagined. Built, in the Palladian style, of pale pink marble, it consisted of a central dome flanked by two smaller ones, to which it was connected by gleaming colonnades. The whole thing was raised above the level of the drive, and approached in the front by a huge twisted marble staircase. Beyond the house there lay a gleaming lake, beyond that again a formal garden of clipped yews, grass and statuary, and in the background of this picture was the pale but piercing blue of a far-distant landscape.

'Good heavens,' said Jasper, when the power of speech returned to him.

'Do you think it beautiful?' said Eugenia. 'I do. I think it is the most beautiful house in the world, but then, of course, I have seen few others.'

'I have never, in any country, seen one to beat it,' said Poppy.

They began to walk slowly towards it.

'Under the Social Unionist régime,' said Jasper, 'your Captain should make a law that all really beautiful houses must be preserved and occupied. It is much the most horrible feature of this age that so many are being destroyed, allowed to stand derelict, or, worst of all, handed over to the proletariat and turned into post-card counters and ice-cream booths. That is too ignoble. Beautiful houses ought to be a setting for beautiful women, their lovers, and perhaps a few frail, but exquisite little children.'

Eugenia looked at him reprovingly. 'Under our régime,' she said, 'women will not have lovers. They will have husbands and great quantities of healthy Aryan children. I think you forget the teachings of our Captain, Union Jackshirt Aspect.'

Poppy St Julien said, 'I don't know a thing about politics, but I'm sure Hitler must be a wonderful man. Hasn't he forbidden German women to work in offices and told them they never need worry about anything again, except arranging the flowers? How they must love him.'

'They do,' said Eugenia. '*Heil Hitler!* Cousin Poppy St Julien, you must be enrolled as a Union Jackshirt at once. It costs ninepence a month, the Union Jack shirt is five shillings, and sixpence for the little emblem. Here we are.'

Vivian Jackson and the Reichshund followed them up the twisted marble staircase, but when they had reached the top a word from Eugenia made them turn round and trot down it again 'Stay there,' she said, over her shoulder, and ushered Poppy and Jasper into a huge domed room, so blue that it might have been a pool in some Mediterranean lagoon, and they fishes swimming in it.

Across its azure immensity sat Lady Chalford waiting to dispense tea out of a golden tea-pot of exquisite design. She looked rather like Whistler's portrait of his mother.

6

If Lady Chalford was like a relic from a forgotten age, a museum-piece of great antiquity, it was not because her years were heavy so much as that her speech, her dress, and her outlook, had remained unaltered since before the War. Nineteen fourteen had marked the evening of her days when she should have been yet in her prime.

The world calamity, however, had little or nothing to do with this decline, having been far eclipsed in her eyes by the disastrous marriage made by her only son; while to her, his death in 1920 from wounds received the day before the Armistice, was a lesser disaster than the fact of his divorce. It made no difference in the eyes of his parents that Lord Malmains had divorced his wife; her shame was his, and theirs, and furthermore the heiress to their lands and titles had the tainted blood of an adulteress in her veins. No such thing had ever happened before in the Malmains family, through-out history no shadow of disgrace had ever fallen upon the proud ambitious heads whose likenesses now stared down from pink brocade walls in Lord Chalford's portrait gallery.

Since the disaster Lady Chalford had never set foot outside her park gates. Lord Chalford, protected by an armour of total deaf-ness, had, until recently laid low by a stroke, performed his duties as a legislator most punctiliously, but when in London he had always stayed at his club, the almost unearthly beauties of Malmains Palace, in Cheyne Walk, having now been hidden from all human eyes, except those of the caretaker, for sixteen long years.

Eugenia had been handed over to her grandparents at the age of three, after her father's death. They could never forgive her for what her mother had been, and regarded the poor child with suspi-cion, which became tempered, however, as she grew older with a sort of sorrowful affection. Luckily, her appearance made things easier for them, Malmains women were all large blonde goddesses, and her looks bore no relation to those of their sinful daughter-in-law. Now that she had reached the age of seventeen she presented a problem with which poor Lady Chalford wrestled miserably. What was to be done with her? Of no use to give her a London season, how should any respectable mother invite, any decent young man propose, to the Child of Scandal. (Lady Chalford, it will be observed, was a trifle pessimistic in her estimate of modern London Society's attitude towards heiresses.) And yet Eugenia must marry, Chalford House and the barony of Malmains which she would in due course inherit from her grandfather must have an heir.

Haunted night and day by these problems, Lady Chalford had been constrained to question Eugenia with regard to the two young strangers whom she had so indiscreetly spoken to on the village green. Had they been suitable friends for the child they would surely have waited to be presented before addressing a young lady, yet, might it be that they had been brought by the hand of a far-seeing Providence to Chalford? She was disposed to consider that such had been the case when she learnt that one of them was Mr Jasper Aspect, grandson, she reassured herself with Debrett, yes, sure enough, grandson of her old friend, Driburgh, and child of that enchantingly pretty little Lady Venetia. Her delight knew no bounds, at last somebody of her own kind, somebody whom she could consult on equal terms, was at hand. Her thoughts sprang happily forward, even should he wish to marry Eugenia the match would be a perfectly suitable one, the Aspects although far from rich, were an old family of unimpeachable antecedents.

Lady Chalford's pleasure at seeing Jasper was greatly, however, surpassed by that which she felt when she realized Poppy's identity. Here was a member of her own family, a married woman and a woman of the world at that; Poppy would certainly be able to advise her what were the best measures to take for her granddaughter's future happiness. She would be able now to talk without the reservations which would have been imposed upon her if she were discussing the case with a gentleman. For the first few moments indeed she did not at all realize the good fortune which had befallen her. She was immensely annoyed with Eugenia for bringing two visitors when only one had been expected. There were a cup and plate too few, another chair must be drawn up. Eugenia's reluctance to invite Marjorie and Noel now became comprehensible, Lady Chalford would fuss herself almost ill over such an incident. When at last they were settled, however, she declared herself overjoyed to see Poppy.

'Agatha's granddaughter,' she cried, embracing her. 'When I was ten years old Agatha and I were inseparable. I remember so well that we both had plum-coloured merino dresses with beautiful brass buttons, the size of pennies, down the front of the bodices. When my poor great-uncle died mamma cut the brass buttons off mine, I was very much displeased by this, having hoped for a proper mourning such as grown-up people had, and besides, I was fond of those buttons – the dress was never much without them. At nineteen Aggie was a most beautiful girl. We went to the same drawing-room and everyone was talking of her beauty. I never shall forget her as a bride. Everybody loved her. Poor Driburgh was so madly in love with her that we feared he should kill himself when she married your dear grandfather. And at twenty-two she was dead. I remember that I heard the news a week after I became engaged myself, and it seemed to take away all my happiness. I think now that she was perhaps fortunate to die so young and still so happy. I am very glad that you have come to see me, my dear child.'

Poppy was moved by this tribute to her grandmother, who, up to now had seemed a most shadowy figure.

'Also I am very much pleased to meet you, Mr Aspect. How is poor dear Driburgh?'

'I believe he is perfectly happy,' said Jasper. 'My mother goes to see him fairly often.'

'Of course Peersmont is a wonderful place,' said Lady Chalford, referring to that lunatic asylum, which, as its name denotes, is kept exclusively for the use of insane peers. 'I often think to myself where should we be without it? To know that our loved ones, in their great trouble, are so perfectly cared for, that indeed is much. You know, I suppose, that it is not at all far from here, in fact I think you ought to visit your dear grandfather. I will be happy to send you over in one of my motor cars if you should wish to do so.'

Jasper thanked her and said he would be glad to avail himself of her kindness. He then began to ask many questions about Chalford House, but was obliged to be content with the vaguest of information, Lady Chalford evidently noticed its beauties no more than the air she breathed.

After tea, however, she said that as Jasper appeared to be so much interested in it, Eugenia might show him the other rooms and the pictures, so long as they were suitably chaperoned by Nanny.

'I wish to have a little talk with dear Poppy,' she said, and presently she conducted Mrs St Julien upstairs to a small boudoir decorated in the Edwardian manner. It was pink and white, like a sugar cake, with white lace over pink satin in panels on the walls. There were two exquisitely comfortable *chaise-longues* upholstered in white brocade edged with pink silk rosebuds, several small pink satin armchairs, each with a blue muslin beribboned cushion, and a quantity of occasional tables covered with albums, photographs of ladies with tremendous eyebrows in straw boaters, and bric-à-brac of every description. Poppy thought she had never seen anything so pretty and so feminine in her life.

During the little talk that followed, Lady Chalford poured out all her misgivings over the future of Eugenia into Poppy's sympathetic ear. 'You see how it is,' she said, 'dear Poppy. Now what should you advise me to do with the poor child?'

'Personally I should be inclined to take her out in London,' said Poppy. 'Everything is so changed there, since the War, and people are by no means as strict as they were.'

'My dear, that may well be the case in certain circles,' said Lady Chalford stiffly. 'Among my own friends, however, and those people with whom I should wish my granddaughter to visit, I am convinced that she would never be received. And even if, out of charity or friendship for me, people did invite her to their houses, it would still be most painful to me. What pleasure could I derive, for instance, from taking the child of a divorced woman to Court? The scandal nearly killed both my husband and myself at the time; with Eugenia making a début in London we must continually be reminded of it. To begin with, neither of us has set foot inside Malmains Palace since the last day of that terrible trial. And then consider what anxiety I should feel in chaperoning her. Eugenia is the child of a bad, wicked woman, never forget that. No, I assure you that it would be impossible for me to take her out in London. My only wish is that she may marry as soon as may be. But whom? This Mr Aspect, now, what should you say are his intentions?'

'Oh, I'm sure he thinks of her as a child,' said Poppy. 'She is so young, isn't she, and young for her age at that. I shouldn't marry her off just yet, Lady Chalford. I think that would be a mistake if I may say so. Why don't you entertain for her down here? Give a garden party, for instance, and perhaps a ball later on, in the autumn. There must be some nice young people in the neighbourhood?'

Lady Chalford considered for a little while and then said: 'This seems to me, dear Poppy, a most excellent plan. I will mention it to my husband this evening, and if he agrees we will give a garden party for the child next month. Now you must promise that you will stay down here and help me, little Poppy. I have not entertained for many years, and we shall want it to be gay. Darling Aggie had the greatest talent for organizing picnics and such things; I vividly remember one enchanting expedition she arranged to a wishing-well, when I wished that I might marry that handsome Mr Howard (I was very young then). But I told my wish to Effie Cholmondely, so of course it never could come true. And then there were always the theatricals at Christmas time. How would it be if we combined something of that sort with our garden party? A pageant, for example – I am told they are tremendously popular nowadays? Then all you young people could take part in it.'

'I think that's a splendid idea,' said Poppy.

'Very well then, we'll see what can be arranged. By the way, where is your husband, my dear?'

Poppy considered it on the whole discreet to say that her husband was delayed in London on business, but that she was expecting him to join her at the Jolly Roger in a few days time.

'My friend, Marjorie Merrith, is there and her maid,' she went on, feeling secure in the assumption that Lady Chalford was no reader of the illustrated daily Press.

'Ah! yes,' said Lady Chalford, 'bring her to see me some time. Poor dear Puggie (her father) was a great friend of my darling Malmains. But, dearest child, is it not rather adventurous for you two young women to be staying quite alone in a country inn? Of course I know the Jolly Roger is a very respectable sort of place, but even so, I feel that it is hardly suitable. Would you not both prefer to move in here until your husband arrives?'

Poppy however, deciding in her own mind that freedom was preferable to comfort, made excuses which Lady Chalford accepted graciously enough. Soon after this Jasper and Eugenia appeared, having finished their tour of the house.

'I think we should be going now,' Poppy said.

When they had left Lady Chalford made her way to her husband's bedroom, and shouting down his ear-trumpet informed him that Poppy was a dear child with wonderfully red lips who reminded her vividly of darling Aggie. 'I only fear,' she added, 'that she may be rather unconventional in some of her habits. She evidently walked home quite alone with young Mr Aspect. I wonder whether I ought to encourage Eugenia in this friendship.' Lord Chalford made no comment. He lay, as always, on his back, staring at the beautiful plaster ceiling high above his bed. Lady Chalford invariably consulted him before taking any decision.

'Perhaps really,' she went on, 'I ought not to invite her here again, perhaps I should give up all idea of this garden party and pageant.'

She sighed, knowing quite well that to do so would be beyond her power. Now that it had once made its appearance that young gay face must often be seen at Chalford House. It had brought a happiness into her life which she had not known for sixteen years, the happiness of talking freely, cosily, and at length to another woman.

Eugenia walked back to the Jolly Roger with her friends. Her animals came too.

Poppy said: 'I think your grandmother is a perfect angel.'

'She is,' said Eugenia, 'I'm fond of the poor old female myself, but I can never forget that she has treated me really very badly. She wouldn't let me go to school, you see, and the result is that I hardly know any Greek at all. I did manage to learn Latin, with the clergyman at Rackenbridge but only after making the most fearful fuss. She never wanted me to.'

'I doubt whether you would have learnt much Greek at school, judging by the perfect illiteracy of the schoolgirls I have met,' said Jasper.

'Then I wanted to go and study National Socialism in Germany, but she stopped me doing that too. She is a great trial to me, the poor old female.'

Poppy told them about the projected garden party, and Lady Chalford's idea of having a pageant at the same time, upon which Eugenia flew into a state of excitement.

'Don't you see,' she cried, 'that this is a most wonderful opportunity for having a grand Social Unionist rally. All the comrades (the Union Jackshirt Comrades, I mean) for miles round, can act in the pageant and help us in every way; they'd love it. Then we will make the people pay to come in and like that will earn a lot of money for the funds.'

'That wasn't quite your grandmother's idea, you know,' said Poppy doubtfully.

'No, of course not, but there's no reason why T.P.O.F. should ever find out, she's very easy to deceive in such ways. I say, the Comrades will be pleased. Union Jackshirt Aspect, I shall count on your support in this matter.'

'You shall have it,' said Jasper.

In the garden of the Jolly Roger they found Noel, who, accompanied by Mrs Lace, was gloomily awaiting their arrival. Noel would have preferred to keep his find to himself for a little longer, but Mrs Lace, having wheedled out of him the true identities of Miss Smith and Miss Jones, absolutely insisted upon meeting them. Lady Marjorie, however, was still reposing on her bed.

The introductions having been effected Mrs Lace became extremely gushing towards Poppy, and waved her hips at Jasper in a most inviting fashion, much to poor Noel's apprehension. Eugenia she evidently regarded as a mere child, beneath her notice. Jasper took an immediate dislike to her, and rudely went on discussing the pageant with Poppy as though they were alone together.

'A pageant?' cried Mrs Lace, when after listening eagerly to them for a few minutes she had gathered what they were talking about. 'In Chalford Park? But this is unheard of. Nobody in the neighbourhood has seen Chalford House since the div— for years and years,' she emended, looking at Eugenia.

'I have never seen it although I live so near. How too exciting. You must be sure and give me a good part in the pageant,' she added archly, 'because I studied acting in Paris, you know, under the great Bernhardt.'

'The great Bottom,' said Jasper, in a loud aside to Poppy.

The others felt that he had gone too far, and Poppy, who was a kind little person, quickly said that of course Mrs Lace must have the chief part.

'You must let me help you with the clothes too,' Mrs Lace went on, looking at Jasper from beneath her eyelashes, 'my nanny and I between us could easily run them up on the sewing-machine, and at Rackenbridge there is a dressmaker who is quite competent.

We might get her to help us cheap if it's for charity. I am sure Mr Aspect would design some beautiful dresses for us.'

'What on earth do you suppose I am?' asked Jasper, highly indignant. 'A pansy dress designer, eh?' Jasper felt that in thus discouraging Mrs Lace he was, as far as Noel was concerned, singing for his supper; he did not perhaps yet quite realize that she was the kind of woman who thrives on kicks and blows.

'If you want actors for crowd scenes and so on I can round up the Women's Institute and put you in touch with every sort of person,' she went on, perfectly unmoved.

It was by now apparent that Mrs Lace was one of those people whose energies, whilst often boring, are occasionally indispensable. Poppy and Jasper recognized though they deplored this fact. Noel sat in a kind of admiring trance.

'Now,' said Mrs Lace briskly, 'we must all lay our heads together and decide what period this pageant is to be.'

'A Pageant of Social Unionism,' said Eugenia at once, 'the March on Rome, the Death of Horst Wessel, the Burning of the Reichstag, the Presidential Election of Roosevelt.'

'Very nice, but don't you think perhaps a trifle esoteric?' said Jasper.

Mrs Lace looked scornfully at Eugenia. 'Pageants,' she said, 'must be historical. Now I suggest Charles I and Henrietta Maria's visit to Chalford – it actually happened, you know. They came to Chalford Old Manor, a perfect little Tudor ruin on the edge of the park.'

Jasper observed that a perfect ruin was a contradiction in terms.

Eugenia vetoed the suggestion of Charles I. 'You can't have Charles and Henrietta Maria at a Social Unionist rally,' she said. 'Cromwell and Mrs Cromwell, if you like – the first Englishman to have the right political outlook.'

'Nobody ever heard of Mrs Cromwell appearing in a pageant,' said Noel. 'It would be simply absurd. Do for goodness' sake stick to the ordinary pageant characters – Edward I, Florence Nightingale, Good Queen Bess, Hengist and Horsa, the Orange Girl of Old Drury,

William Rufus, Sir Philip Sidney, or Rowena, otherwise you'll find yourselves getting into a fearful muddle.'

'Oh! I don't agree with you at all,' said Mrs Lace, thinking thus to curry favour with Jasper. 'Do let's be original, whatever happens.'

Poppy, seeing that the discussion was about to become acrimonious, put an end to it by reminding the others that the idea of a pageant had originated with Lady Chalford, and that therefore it would be a matter of ordinary politeness to let her choose its period. Eugenia said that she must now return home as T.P.O.F. would scold her for going to Chalford with the others if it were found out. *'Heil Hitler!'* she cried, and swinging herself on to the back of Vivian Jackson she galloped away.

'Poor little thing, what a bore she is with her stupid Movement,' said Mrs Lace spitefully.

'Oh, dear, how I do disagree with you,' said Jasper. 'Personally I can't imagine a more fascinating girl. If all débutantes were like that I should never be away from Pont Street during the summer months.'

'Such awful clothes,' said Mrs Lace angrily.

'Are they? I really hadn't noticed. In the face of such staggering beauty I suppose little details of that sort are likely to escape one.'

'And all that Social Unionist nonsense.'

'Nonsense, is it?' cried Jasper. 'Perhaps you are not aware, Madam, that Social Unionism is now sweeping the world as Liberalism swept the world of the eighteenth century. You call it nonsense – in spite of the fact that millions of people are joyfully resigning themselves to its sway. Pray now let us have an attack on the principles of Social Unionism delivered from a standpoint of sense.'

Mrs Lace did not take refuge in silence as a lesser woman might have done. She tossed her head and pronounced that when you find schoolgirls like Eugenia going mad about something you can be pretty sure that it is nonsense.

'I'm afraid I don't follow your argument. On the contrary,

I believe that Eugenia belongs to a new generation which is going to make a new and better and a cleaner world for old back numbers like you and me to end our days in.'

Mrs Lace winced at this, but returned gallantly to the charge. 'I am sure we must be very well off as we are. Why do you want to have a lot of changes in the Government of this country?'

'My dear good Mrs Lace, you must have been keeping company with the local Conservative M.P. Captain Chadlington, I believe, has the honour of representing this part of the world (and a more congenital half-wit never breathed).'

Mrs Lace was not altogether displeased by this allegation. Captain Chadlington and his wife, Lady Brenda, constituted, in fact, a peak of social ambition which she had recently conquered.

'Well?' she said, 'and then?'

'I suppose that poor baboon has been telling you that we are very well off as we are? Very well off, indeed! I don't ask you to look at the unemployment figures which are a commonplace. I do point to the lack of genius to be found in the land, whether political, artistic, or literary. I point with scorn to our millionaires, who, not daring to enjoy their wealth, cower in olde worlde cottages, and hope that no one will suspect them of being rich; to the city man grubbing his ill-gotten money in the hopes of achieving this dreary aim, and unable to take an interest in anything but market prices or golf; to the aristocrats who, as Eugenia truly says, prefer the comfort of a luxury flat to the hardship of living on their own land; to the petty adulteries, devoid of passion, which are indulged in by all classes, and to the cowardly pacifism which appears to be the spirit of the age. Nothing grand, nothing individual, nothing which could make anybody suppose that the English were once a fine race, brave, jolly and eccentric. So I say that we need a new spirit in the land, a new civilization, and it is to the Eugenias of this world that I look for salvation. Perhaps that new spirit is called Social Unionism, in any case let us leave no stone unturned. Our need is desperate, we must hail any movement which may relight the spark of vitality in this nation before it is too late, anything which may save us from the paralysing squalor, both mental and moral, from which we are suffering so terribly at present. Germany and Italy have been saved by National Socialism; England might be saved by Social Unionism, who can tell? Therefore I say, *"Heil Hitler!" "Viva il Duce!"*, and "Miss" – Miss, I'll have another beer, please.'

7

Lady Marjorie Merrith leant back in the bath that was, so disturbingly, not built in, and covered her smooth white arms with lacy sleeves of soap.

'You must admit that it's tiresome of them,' she said to Poppy who, faithful to her rôle of confidante, was perched on a chair beside the bath. 'After all, I particularly said in both my notes that any communications would be forwarded by my bank, and besides, they could easily have found out where we are by now, if they had really wanted to. I do think they might show some sign of life – makes it so awkward for me. What is my next move?'

'Really, darling, you must decide these things for yourself. It all depends on whether or not you want to marry Osborne – which is it?'

Marjorie said with petulance that she didn't know. 'I ran away,' she continued angrily, 'to find romance, and I have only found this disgusting bath.'

'Well, I don't know what you expect. There are two quite presentable young men staying in this very hotel, much more than you could have hoped for.'

'I don't like them.'

'I never shall understand how you could have left that gorgeous wedding dress.'

'Well, you know, I have an idea that the fashions will be far prettier next winter. What d'you suppose poor mummie is doing with the presents?'

'Keeping them, of course. After all the engagement isn't broken off in *The Times*, remember; you've got scarlet-fever. I must say I take off my hat to your mother for thinking of that, it lasts six weeks you know, and at the end of that time, if you want to, you will be able to break off your engagement without the smallest scandal. People are far too busy laying each other out in Venice at this time of year to think about your affairs. The duke is evidently playing for time; you won't have to make up your mind until the hospital trains begin arriving at Victoria after the hols.'

'Yes, but now what,' said Lady Marjorie, running in some more hot water. She yelled to make herself heard above the noise, 'I can't stay in this lousy hole all the summer.'

'I can't see why not.'

'It's not quite my dish, darling, now is it?'

'When you come to think of it this pub isn't at all uncomfortable, and you couldn't fail to find the local life wildly entertaining if only you would throw yourself into it more.'

'I can't do that you see. I don't like any of the people, except, of course, Eugenia.'

'Hate them then. Do you a lot of good. You've never hated anyone in your life, or loved anyone either. You don't know the meaning of real emotion, and that's why you can't make up your mind about the duke.'

'I love you,' said Lady Marjorie.

'Well, I think perhaps you do,' said Poppy, 'there's nothing radically wrong with your nature, darling, but your upbringing and environment, so far, have been lousy. I never met anybody more unfitted to cope with the ordinary contingencies of life – especially the emotional side of it.'

'Would you marry Osborne?'

'I've told you a thousand times. These vague romantic impulses won't do anybody any good, and least of all yourself, it's not as though you had any real reason for breaking it off. If I were you I should go straight home and say you're sorry.'

'I don't exactly mean would you marry him if you were me. I mean would you marry him if you were you?'

'Well, I suppose I would. He's a duke, and I should have a diamond tiara, very nice.'

'But if he wasn't a duke?'

'My darling Marge, the whole thing about Osborne is that he *is* a duke. People can't be divorced from their status in life like that. You might as well say if George Robey wasn't an actor, or if Hitler wasn't a Führer. They just wouldn't be Hitler or George Robey, that's all.'

'No I suppose they wouldn't. Then we stay here do we?'

'Oh! let's. I tell you this village is a highly interesting place just at present. Besides, I'm enjoying my flip with Mr Aspect a whole heap.'

'Poppy.'

'Mm.'

'Aren't you still in love with Anthony?'

'Oh – in love. I don't really know. I'm extremely angry with him at present, but as for love —'

'Does he want to marry the girl do you think?'

'God knows what Anthony wants, ever. If he doesn't marry her I can promise you that he'll be eating out of my hand again in a few months time. He always comes drearily trundling back to me after these little incidents. But this time I don't feel at all certain that I'll take him back. I believe it would be better to make a clean break at last. Sometimes I think I really can't stand it any longer. You see, supposing he comes back now, fearfully penitent, and rather sweet as he always is, the whole routine will be certain to start again before long. About the beginning of next season, I should think, he will be falling for some awful little débutante, and she'll have to be in my house morning, noon, and night, with me always about the place as a suitable chaperone. The girl will hate me, because the poor little fool will suppose that I am the only obstacle to her eternal happiness, and I shall be bored into fits by her idiotic chatter. If only he would choose rather more companionable ones I might be able to bear it, or if he would have a straightforward affair with a married woman in her own house – these sentimental attachments to little girls in mine are so humiliating. Really, now I come to think of it, I'm absolutely sick and tired of Anthony St Julien.'

'Poor sweet. And you're still in love with him, aren't you?' said

Lady Marjorie, slowly emerging from her bath into the towel which Poppy was holding out for her.

'I suppose I am, really. I've got into the habit of being in love with him, and you know how hard it is breaking oneself of habits.'

Jasper and Noel meanwhile were sitting in the bar drinking beer, which they fondly supposed would give them an appetite for the joint of beef whose luscious odours were at that very moment floating about the passage, stairs, and landing of the Jolly Roger.

'Jasper, old boy,' said Noel, who was in a particularly expansive mood, 'I really think you might have been nicer to Anne-Marie. She was most awfully upset after you had pitched into her like that over Social Unionism the other day. I told her you didn't mean a word of what you said, but that you would always take up any standpoint for the sake of an argument.'

'And that's not strictly true either. I believe a great deal of what I said, and if I were in any way politically minded, which I'm not, I should most certainly join the Social Unionist Movement.'

'You have, old boy.'

'Splendid, so I have. So have you. Fine girl, Eugenia. Incidentally you're not making much headway with your bride-to-be, are you?'

'I've decided that Eugenia can keep,' said Noel carelessly. 'She doesn't look much like a marrying girl to me at present, a few months one way or the other won't make all that difference, and in any case I'm potty about Anne-Marie. Don't you agree that she is an exquisite beauty?'

'She's all right,' said Jasper. 'Too bitchy for me though. And why full evening dress at tea-time?'

'It wasn't full evening dress you idiot, it was a little beach frock.'

'Well, I reckon we must be a hundred good miles from the nearest beach.'

'You don't seem to understand, Jasper. That child never has any fun, never goes to Venice or the South of France like other girls of her age. So, in order to make her life seem more interesting she has to make believe all the time, poor darling.'

'Like Mrs Thompson you mean?'

'I've a very good mind to take her off to Cannes with me next week.'

'My dear old boy, now, for God's sake don't lose your head. There's the husband remember.'

'You don't have to remind me,' said Noel, moodily. 'And from what I hear I should think he's the divorcing kind too. Sounds a perfect swine. Poor little Anne-Marie, you have no idea what that child has to put up with.'

'Oh, well, you can have lots of fun down here. Just think of the pageant, garden party, and Grand Social Unionist rally, it will be a perfect riot. Besides, like this you can keep an eye on Eugenia, which seems to me an exceedingly important feature from your point of view, eh what?

'I say, old boy,' he added, half rising in his seat and staring out of the window, 'just come here and take a look at these two chaps would you?' Noel looked without much interest. Two excessively ordinary men in tweed coats and grey flannel trousers stood outside the Jolly Roger. Two suitcases, which clearly belonged to them, were being removed from a hired car by the boot-boy, and deposited in the hall.

'This pub will be overflowing soon,' remarked Noel, in a bored kind of voice.

'Private detective agents,' said Jasper.

'Good heavens! Jasper, do you really think so?'

'I know it.'

'How?'

'By the look of them for one thing. Nobody looks quite so obtrusively ordinary as private detective agents. Besides I'm practically certain the left-hand one is the chap who used to shadow poor little Marigold. She got awfully chummy with him after a bit, allowed him to keep a charcoal brazier inside her garden gate when the weather got bad, and promised to stay at home all Christmas Day so that he could spend it with his kiddies. He liked her a lot after that.'

'Who can they be after down here?'

'That's what I propose to find out, it's an exceedingly important point because you see it might be any one of us.'

'I don't see why.'

'Well, my dear old boy, just consider the situation for a moment. Major Lace, to begin with yourself, may well be feeling jealous; Mr St Julien would be only human if he was wondering why his wife came to this unlikely place; the Duke of Dartford is probably not uninterested in getting the low-down on Lady Marjorie's behaviour here, while it is not beyond the bounds of possibility that my Uncle Bradenham may be beginning to guess at the authorship of certain blackmailing letters which he receives from time to time (only when I am on my beam ends, of course, and anyway the old miser jolly well ought to make me a decent allowance).'

'This is too fearful,' said Noel. 'What are we to do?'

'I'm going to send for the girls, warn them about these dicks, and evolve some plan of action.'

Jasper sent a note up to Poppy's room, with the boots, who had finished carrying luggage. In it he requested that she and Lady Marjorie should join him in the bar as soon as they were up and dressed.

'You'd better come along Marge,' said Poppy, as her friend began to demur at this suggestion. 'I told you before, you must join in the life here unless you want to die of boredom.'

'I shall probably be rude to Mr Aspect.'

'That's all right, he'll give as good as he gets. Don't you worry about him.'

'Good morning,' said Jasper, as they walked into the bar a few minutes later. 'What's yours?'

'What's what?' said Lady Marjorie.

'I meant to say that as we are having the unexpected pleasure of your company, my dear lady (running a bit short of face cream, I suppose?) what can we offer you in the shape of a drink? You so rarely assume a vertical position in these days that I imagine you to be in need of alcoholic support when you do.'

'Thank you,' said Lady Marjorie coldly. 'I have been brought up to regard drinking in between meals as a very middle-class habit.'

'I see, you prefer to get sozzled in the dining-room, I suppose. What's yours, Miss Smith?'

Poppy said she would like a glass of sherry, and after this had duly been procured Jasper proceeded to impart his news.

'Now the point is,' he said, 'that they may be after any one of us, and it would really be a good thing if we could find out which. The sooner the better in fact, so what we must have now is a little intelligent co-operation. I suggest that after luncheon today Miss Smith here, Noel, and myself, should each go for a long walk in different directions. Lady Marjorie, having lost, it appears, the use of her legs, had better spread a pot of "Ponds" over her face and resume horizontality. Now private detective agents always behave in a pathetically obvious way, and whichever one of us it is that they are after will certainly find him or herself shadowed by these boys. However fast, however tirelessly one walks, it is impossible to shake them off. On the other hand, if they stay around here we can set our minds at rest. It will only mean that old Dartford is keeping an eye on those gold and diamond hair brushes, and so on.'

'How dare you go into my bedroom?' said Lady Marjorie, with cold fury.

'My dear lady, I didn't have to go into it. The door happened to be wide open and I was positively blinded by the flashing of gems which came from your dressing-table. Why, I nearly fell down the stairs.'

Poppy giggled at this.

Lady Marjorie gave her a reproving look, and saying: 'I think you are a very rude and badly-brought-up young man, Mr Aspect, and I think all this nonsense about detectives is simply childish,' she left the bar.

'That's all right,' said Jasper. 'We can count on her for complete immobility during the afternoon – lend her your face cream, Miss Smith, in case she's run out, would you? What about you then, are you falling in with my scheme?'

Poppy said that it was all rather Phillips Oppenheim, but she supposed there could be no harm in it.

They arranged, after a good deal of talk, that Jasper should wander round to Comberry Manor at about four o'clock, and pay a call on Mrs Lace.

Poppy had already promised that she would take tea with Lady Chalford in order to discuss the garden party and pageant, so she would stick to that plan. This would leave Noel to await Eugenia, who was to be at the twopenny-bar shop as usual.

'Common sense demands that we should begin by allaying any possible suspicion until we see how the land lies,' said Jasper. 'For instance, if I go to Comberry Manor, they will be put off the scent as far as Noel and Mrs Lace are concerned —'

'But there is nothing,' Noel interrupted. 'I mean I have only seen Mrs Lace about three times in my life.'

'Still, you're mad about the girl, and intend to see her a good deal more in future. By this time next week there's no knowing what won't have happened, eh, old boy? To continue, Miss Smith can go with the utmost propriety and visit her second cousin four times removed, or whatever it is, neither could there be any harm in Noel smoking a pipe on the village green, or in Lady Marjorie's virginal cultivation of beauty, a pursuit in which, as everybody knows, she constantly indulges. I consider, ladies and gentlemen, that it is exceedingly important for us to find out which pole these boys are barking up. Once we know that we shall doubtless be able to thwart them at every turn.'

8

It was another day of intense heat, the sky was deep indigo, the shadows beneath the trees were black. No birds sang, and the landscape quivered slightly. Poppy, as she walked towards Chalford House, felt extremely contented. She was at her best in hot weather, it suited her and made her feel energetic. This was the first summer she had spent in England for some years, and she thought that nowhere abroad had she seen such beautiful days. The little coppice through which the drive passed just after the lodge gates was very dark, and smelt deliciously of leaf-mould, and the hot bark of trees. Chalford House itself, lying in a dancing haze of heat, looked like three enormous pink pearls upon a green velvet cushion. Eugenia now came into the picture, riding lazily upon a sleeping Vivian Jackson, and bound, no doubt, for the twopenny-bar shop.

'T.P.O.F. is expecting you,' she cried. 'Hail and farewell, cousin Poppy St Julien.'

'Hail and farewell, Eugenia,' said Poppy smiling. A moment later she turned and shouted over her shoulder, 'Noel is waiting for you on the village green.'

Lady Chalford received her with an almost touching cordiality. 'Dear child,' she cried, 'I have been thinking of you a great deal since Thursday – it is a very happy thing for me that you have come to Chalford. Why, I have not seen one of my relations since our tragedy – sixteen years ago. You must tell me a great deal of news – first of all, how is your dear mother?'

Poppy said that her dear mother was very well. She did not mention the painful fact that they had not been on speaking terms since Poppy's marriage to Anthony St Julien. Lady Chalford then proceeded to inquire after innumerable collaterals, mentioning aunts, uncles, and cousins, of whose existence Poppy was, in many cases, hardly herself aware.

'Dear child,' Lady Chalford said, when Poppy was unable to throw any light on the health, happiness, or even the whereabouts of two of her own father's first cousins, 'you seem to be, as a family, sadly *décousu*, if I may say so.'

The old lady evidently carried in her head a vast family tree, not a birth, a death, or a marriage among the remotest of her connections seemed ever to have escaped her notice. Poppy thought it a sad thing that her extraordinary prejudice against so normal an eventuality as the fact of a divorce should have caused her to be shut away for ever from the world. She was evidently a woman who possessed an unusual capacity for affection and interest in the lives of other people.

They began to talk about the garden party, Lady Chalford producing a list of those neighbours who had been invited to her son's coming-of-age ball in 1912. 'I expect it must be a little out of date now,' she said, smiling. 'I must try and get it revised before the invitations are sent. There is no hurry really.' She then suggested a date for the party in about three weeks' time. 'Will that give you long enough to get up a little pageant, dear?'

'Oh! yes,' said Poppy, 'if we get to work straight away. Will you settle a subject for the pageant? As soon as that is fixed we can get on with it.'

'I was thinking about that before you came,' said Lady Chalford. 'Now two monarchs, with their wives, are known to have visited Chalford, so we shall be able to repeat actual history itself. They were Charles the First and Henrietta Maria, who came to the Old Manor, and George the Third and Queen Charlotte. They came to see Chalford House when it was finally completed, and I incline myself towards reproducing their visit, for this reason. We still have, in the stables here, George the Third's own coach, and I thought it would be very interesting to use that for the scene of his arrival. Those acting the parts of King George and Queen Charlotte could get into the coach somewhere behind the kitchen garden, drive round the park and then up to the house – if you will come to this window, dear, I will show you exactly how it can be arranged.' She led Poppy forward and began pointing out various landmarks and a route for the coach. Poppy, however, was paying no attention to her. For, standing in the middle of the drive, looking up at Chalford House, were two excessively ordinary men in tweed jackets and grey flannel trousers. Poppy gazed at them for a moment, thunderstruck, then inadvertently cried out, 'Oh! Anthony, you dirty swine!' Lady Chalford turned towards her in amazement. Putting an arm round her waist she said, 'Dear Poppy, you are very white. Come and lie down for a little, it is the heat – you should never have walked all the way from the village. I will send at once for my motor car to take you home again.'

The local beauty looked out of her drawing-room window and saw Jasper Aspect coming towards the house. He ignored the drive, which twisted and turned among rhododendron bushes like a snake in its death agony (a late Victorian arrangement calculated to make the grounds seem more spacious), and strode carelessly over lawn and flower-beds alike, until, reaching the front door, he gave a tremendous peal to the bell. Mrs Lace meanwhile had escaped to her bedroom. She was delighted by this very unexpected turn of circumstance; she thought Jasper far more attractive than the too-obviously infatuated Noel, but had rather given up hope of his conquest since their meeting at the Jolly Roger. Telling her maid that she would be down in a moment, she hastily proceeded to change her clothes, and her face. Anne-Marie Lace was one of those women who alternate in appearance between the very extremes of squalor and smartness; when she was alone she could never be bothered to brush her hair, varnish her nails, or powder her nose; when in company she was always excessively well turned out. Having now arranged herself to her own satisfaction, she came into the drawing-room so quietly that Jasper who, more from habit than interest, was reading a letter he had found on the writing-table, gave a guilty start. Mercifully, however, Mrs Lace appeared to notice nothing, and greeted him with effusion.

'This is nice of you,' she cried, *enchantée de vous voir*,' and she proceeded to sweep about the room in a highly theatrical manner, patting up cushions and tidying away books and newspapers with a variety of stunning gestures. These antics put Jasper in mind of some actress who is left alone on the stage for a few moments after the curtain has gone up.

'That's better now,' she said, smiling at him with wide-opened eyes, 'my little darlings have been romping in here, and you know how children upset everything in a room. Won't you sit down and have a cigarette?' She lit one for him, which gave her another excuse for some highly theatrical gestures.

'Now,' she said, 'we can have a nice cosy gossip. There are so many things I have been longing to ask you, but you weren't very kind to me last time we met.'

'Ah! but we were talking politics then,' said Jasper, as though to imply that more personal topics were now about to be broached. 'But what is it you wanted to ask me?'

'To begin with, what exactly persuaded you and Noel to come down to poor dead-alive old Chalford? That naughty Noel is always so vague about it when I ask him.'

'I expect he is,' said Jasper.

'You know, Mr Aspect, I am very fond of Noel and I'm afraid he is the tiniest little bit in love with me, but —'

'But what?' Jasper thought that in his whole career he had never had sex appeal thrown at his head more deliberately or with less effect. He was profoundly unattracted by Mrs Lace, and decided that it would be a generous and inexpensive gesture if he made a present of her to Noel, lock, stock and barrel.

Mrs Lace continued, 'Well, I don't think I could ever fall for someone like Noel, although he's most awfully sweet, isn't he?'

'Why couldn't you fall for him?'

'I suppose it's because he is so – so indefinite.'

'Perhaps it may be difficult for him, in the circumstances, to be very definite,' said Jasper, wrapping up Mrs Lace in a brown paper parcel, as it were, before handing her over, once and for all, to his friend.

'How do you mean?'

'Perhaps his position, at the moment, is a bit equivocal.'

Mrs Lace wrinkled her forehead and gazed inquiringly at Jasper.

'But, of course, you have guessed long ago.'

'I should very much like to know for certain,' said Mrs Lace, who naturally had no idea at all of Jasper's meaning.

'It is impossible, without a breach of confidence, to tell you everything. The most that I am permitted to say is that if you think you have an idea of whom he really is, you are probably right.'

'Oh!' cried Mrs Lace. She said no more; her brain was in a turmoil. After all, she thought with wild exhilaration, Miss Smith was not Miss Smith, neither was Miss Jones Miss Jones; on the contrary, they were both well-known figures in London Society. Why then should not the name of 'Noel Foster' also conceal some thrilling identity?

'I can see that, of course, you know quite well,' said Jasper, smiling. 'Those famous features are not so easy to disguise, are they? And now, dear Mrs Lace, one word of warning. Don't let the – don't let HIM see that you know. He is down here with the express intention of avoiding publicity, formality, and all the tedious attributes of his position, and if his identity were to be found out, even by the lady whom he – (do you mind if I am frank with you?) whom he so passionately admires, he would leave at once. It would be better if neither of us were to speak of this again, even to each other, and, of course, I rely upon your absolute discretion as far as the outside world is concerned. Should his whereabouts be discovered we should have journalists and photographers behind every tree, and these few short weeks of privacy which he so badly needs would be ruined for him.'

'I will keep his secret locked in my heart for ever,' whispered Mrs Lace, her eyes shining.

'And now the time has come for me to fulfil my errand,' said

Jasper, looking furtively over his shoulder and lowering his voice, 'where can the – where can my friend see you for a while alone and without fear of interruption.'

Mrs Lace, her colour heightening, considered. At last she said, 'In Chalford Park, not so very far from the Old Manor, there is a small lake on whose shores a pink and white temple stands. It is almost entirely overgrown with ivy, honeysuckle and amaryllis, and is concealed from view by the wild-rose bushes which surround it. Nobody ever goes there.'

'Ah! happy Noel,' cried Jasper gallantly. 'With how much envy do I contemplate his lot. Will you, then, be there tomorrow afternoon at three o'clock punctually, and when you hear the hooting of an owl answer with the cry of a woodpecker if you are certain that the coast is clear?'

'Yes, you can count upon it,' said Mrs Lace. Unversed in ornithology she resolved that at dinner she would learn from Major Lace, who was, the cry of the woodpecker.

Jasper now rose and, with a courtly gesture, he kissed her hand prior to taking his leave. At that moment, however, Major Lace could be heard banging about in the hall, and Anne-Marie, who enjoyed showing off her friends to him, begged Jasper to stay a few moments. 'He always complains if people leave as soon as he comes in.'

Major Lace, it appeared, had been attending a sale of pedigree cows. His usually good-humoured face was clouded with extreme bad temper, as, he had, during the sale, turned over by mistake two pages of the catalogue instead of one, and had thus been misled as to the cow for which he was bidding. He bought the wrong one for an exorbitant price only to discover that his purchase was totally lacking in that desirable piece of anatomy – the udder.

'It appears that this brute is well known at sales,' he cried angrily. 'They've been hawking her round the country for months in the hope of finding some mug who would buy her. Chap next to me said, "Why the hell have you bought that cow, Lace?" I said, "Why not? Good cow, good pedigree, heavy record." "Some mistake there, Lace," he said, "her pedigree is all right, but she'll never have a record. Brute is bagless." Then I found out what I'd done, see, turned over two pages of the b— catalogue at once. There was such a glare, you know.'

'Very easy thing to do,' said Jasper sympathetically.

'Damned stupid of me all the same. I should have taken a good look at the brute, then it would never have happened. Bagless she is, absolutely bagless. Have a whisky and soda, Aspect?'

Jasper liked Major Lace. When they had drunk several whiskies he accompanied him round his cow-byres and pigsties and they exchanged dirty stories. Major Lace, who had a jolly, bawdy mind, thought that Jasper was distinctly a cut above Anne-Marie's usual friends, and was soon restored to a good temper.

As for Mrs Lace she slept but little that night. She was tormented with curiosity to know more about Noel, and quite unable to see how this could be achieved. She racked her brains, trying to recall the physiognomy of some royal person who might remotely resemble him. Then it occurred to her that he was perhaps a film star of enormous fame. In any case, he was clearly not unworthy of her chariot wheels, and this thought did much to restore her peace of mind.

No sooner had Jasper left the Jolly Roger and walked off in the direction of Comberry Manor, than Noel began to fall into a shocking state of restlessness. He cursed himself bitterly for consenting to any arrangement whereby Jasper was to enjoy a prolonged tête-à-tête with Mrs Lace; the full horror of the jealous torments he himself would be condemned to endure had not assailed him until the moment when he saw Jasper swinging jauntily down the village street. Dreadful thoughts now came to discomfort him. Jasper was notorious as a seducer of women, and had never shown himself averse to scoring off an old friend if the occasion presented; moreover, Mrs Lace had already shown an obvious predilection for him. Worst of all, she had by no means succumbed, as yet, to Noel's own blandishments, and he greatly feared that she found him uninteresting. He sat gloomily biting his nails, once indeed so desperate did he feel that he started up and made a move to pursue Jasper, but remembering that it was of the utmost importance to find out the motives of the two detectives, and having no wish to cut a jealous figure of fun in the eyes of Jasper and Mrs Lace, he forced himself to remain where he was. He hung about the village in a terrible state of nerves, trying to console himself with the consideration of Jasper's alleged love for Poppy St Julien and his own slight financial hold over Jasper. Neither of these facts afforded him much reassurance.

Presently Eugenia appeared on the scene and talked to him for a little while, but she seemed disappointed not to have found Jasper, whom she evidently regarded as a more satisfactory Social Unionist than Noel. She then busily set to work arranging an empty cottage, whose key she had wheedled out of her grandfather's estate agent, as a Union Jackshirt head-quarters for Chalford and district. Exquisite Chippendale furniture, smuggled away from Chalford House, was being pushed and banged into rooms and through doorways several sizes too small for it. Two or three of the Comrades were working like beavers at this task, while Eugenia stood by to encourage and occasionally to lend her own not inconsiderable weight. Her Nanny also hovered round with a duster, flicking at the pieces which were already in place, and muttering to herself about what her ladyship would say if she knew of such goings on. When the head-quarters were ready (that is, when all the furniture had been forced into position, regardless of chips and knocks, and the rooms had been hung with life-size photographs of Hitler, Mussolini, Roosevelt and the Captain), Eugenia mounted a particularly fragile and valuable settee, which bent beneath her weight, and announced that there was to be a public ceremony for the opening of Chalford's new head-quarters the following Wednesday at 3.30 p.m.

'Well, how was it?' asked Noel, in an agony of suspense, 'did you like Anne-Marie – did she like you – what did you talk about – how did you hit it off together?'

'We got on like a house on fire,' said Jasper. 'Fine girl, Mrs Lace.'
Noel almost groaned out loud. Jasper saw at once what a state of
mind he was in, and found it not unamusing. 'Come and have a
drink at the New Moon,' he said, deciding to prolong the agony
for a bit. 'They ought to be open any minute now.'

'What a perfectly delightful husband she has too,' he continued,
as they nestled up against the bar while waiting for their beer.
'A really charming man. He told me some exceedingly funny
stories. I expect I shall be seeing a great deal of him in the future.'

Noel found this news far from reassuring. He knew that Jasper
always made a point of being on most friendly terms with husbands.

Jasper now changed the subject lightly. He asked whether Noel
had met Eugenia, how she was, and what she had been up to. 'Have
a jolly afternoon yourself?' he inquired. 'Any sign of the dicks? No?
They certainly weren't following me either. Looks like it's one of
those Janes they're after. I wonder which?'

They now gulped their beer in silence. Noel had a dozen questions on the tip of his tongue, and racked his brain to think of
some way in which he could word them without appearing ridiculous. He looked quite pathetic, as though he might burst into
tears at any minute.

Presently Jasper threw him a crumb of comfort.

'Mrs Lace talked a lot about you,' he said.

Noel looked overjoyed for a moment, but this expression soon
gave way to one of apprehension. He felt it more than likely that
the conversation as directed by Jasper might have been on extremely
unflattering lines, uncertain as he was of Mrs Lace's attitude
towards himself. He rather expected that he would be thrown into
a pit of despair by Jasper's next remark. Bracing himself as for a
physical shock he took a large gulp of beer and said: 'Oh! really,
what did she say?'

The crumb of comfort, however, was most unexpectedly
succeeded by the contents of a whole baker's shop.

'Mrs Lace is nuts about you, old boy. She can't think of anything
else.'

Noel still suspected a trap. Walking warily, he said: 'I don't believe she is at all. She never shows it when she is with me, anyway.'

'My dear old boy, you are such a shocking bad psychologist. Can't you realize that Mrs Lace is one of those shy, retiring little women who must have all the running made for them? Haven't you noticed, for one thing, how reserved she is?'

Even the love-blinded Noel had not quite noticed this. He was only too prepared, however, to believe it.

'Never mind,' continued Jasper, 'I think everything should be all right now. I've done a lot of work for you today, old boy. You should be grateful to me.'

'What work?' asked Noel, dubiously.

'To begin with I praised you up to the skies, said you had an exceedingly noble character, and so on. But what is even more important, I made an assignation for you.'

'Not with Anne-Marie?'

'Who else? You are to meet her in a place where you will be quite undisturbed for as long as you wish – a romantic place, a place which might have been (probably was) designed for lovers' meetings. There she will be awaiting your declaration at three o'clock tomorrow afternoon.'

'Where is it then?' cried Noel, who was duly thrown, as Jasper had intended that he should be, into a fever of excited anticipation. 'Quickly, tell me, Jasper, where?'

Jasper did not reply. He appeared to have gone off into a reverie and sat gazing into the middle distance, a dreamy expression on his face.

'Jasper – where is this place, damn you?'

'By the way, old boy,' said Jasper, suddenly coming back to earth again, 'I could do with ten pounds.'

'I dare say you could,' said Noel.

There was a long silence.

'Oh, I see,' said Noel peevishly, 'blackmail?'

'I say, hold on old boy, that's not a very polite word is it? Supposing we called it commission? After all, a chap must live you know.'

'I really can't see why,' said Noel.

Presently however, he pulled out a cheque-book and proceeded with bad grace to scribble a cheque for ten pounds. He then screwed it up in a ball and threw it at Jasper's head. Jasper smoothed it out carefully and read it. 'It's exceedingly untidy,' he said, 'but I dare say it will do.

'Temple by lake near Chalford Old Manor. You approach it hooting like an owl to prove *bona fide*; if all is O.K. Mrs Lace replies with a merry laugh. Let's go back to our pub, shall we, and find out what those girls have been up to all the afternoon.'

Lady Marjorie and Mrs St Julien, however, made no further appearance that evening. They dined, as usual, in their private sitting-room, but after dinner they did not, as was their custom, wander out into the garden to breathe the cool night air before going to bed. They remained in their sitting-room, and were evidently talking nineteen to the dozen. Jasper spent much of his evening with his ear glued to the keyhole, thus balking the detectives who were wandering about like ghosts, apparently with the same intention.

When, very much later than usual, Mrs St Julien retired to her own room, she was slightly startled to notice a figure tucked up comfortably in her bed. It was Jasper's.

'Quite all right,' he said. 'Those boys saw me go into Lady Marjorie's room – I went in there first and then climbed round by the window. Pathetically easy to deceive, dicks are, and as it's you they're after it can't matter to her.'

Poppy St Julien sat down on the chair in front of her dressing-table and looked at him severely. 'Now I wonder how you happen to know it's me they're after – it almost looks as though you must have been listening to my conversation with Marge just now.'

'That's right,' said Jasper, rearranging the pillows so that his head should be on a higher level.

'You appear very ignorant of ordinary social conventions.'

'Perhaps I prefer to ignore them.'

Poppy began to brush her hair.

'I thought,' said Jasper, 'by your tone of voice just now, that you seemed to be upset by Anthony St Julien's behaviour. I am sorry.'

Poppy continued to brush her hair.

'He also prefers to ignore social conventions, it seems.'

'He does,' said Poppy gloomily; 'but there's some excuse for him, poor sweet. He's in love.'

'So am I in love.'

'So you say. But you are such a liar, aren't you? And I wish you wouldn't drop cigarette ash into my bed.'

'Give me an ash-tray then would you, darling Miss Smith? That soap-dish would do. Thanks awfully. Will you marry me?'

'Don't be silly.'

'Silly's my middle name. I asked you a question, however, and should like an answer.'

'Please leave my room.'

'Don't be governessy.'

'I want to undress.'

'Undress then.'

'Oh! damn you,' said Poppy.

'Now look here, Miss Smith darling,' said Jasper, 'do be sensible and listen to me for a minute. Anthony St Julien is an eel and he doesn't want you any more because he lusts after strange débutantes, I am not an eel and I do want you, and I will never leave you for anybody else as long as I live. Now if you marry me everyone will be pleased, Anthony St Julien, his débutante, the detectives, and me. Doesn't it seem an easy way to give pleasure all round?'

'You can't keep me,' said Poppy, 'in the comfort to which I have been accustomed.'

'Same to you, my angel.'

'I dare say, but wives aren't expected to keep their husbands.'

'I never could see why not. It seems so unfair.'

'Not at all. The least the chaps can do is to provide for us financially when you consider that we women have all the trouble of pregnancy and so on.'

'Well, us boys have hang overs don't we? Comes to the same thing in the end.'

'Anyway, the fact remains that I can't keep you and you can't keep me. You ought to be marrying Marge.'

'I know. I would like a shot if I thought there was the smallest chance. Is there?'

'None whatever.'

'There you are. I knew there wasn't. Why raise my hopes? You see, looks like it'll have to be you after all, darling Miss Smith. I can't say I mind much. You are most awfully pretty you know.'

'Jolly kind of you to say so,' said Poppy, yawning. She began to undress.

9

The opening ceremony of Chalford head-quarters happened to fall upon the same day as that of a cocktail-party for which Mrs Lace had sent out invitations. As the one entertainment was billed to take place at 3.30 p.m. and the other not until 6 o'clock, it was evident that both could easily be attended. Anne-Marie's party was ostensibly inaugurated to set in motion the machinery of the pageant. An organizing committee was to be elected and the allocation of minor rôles to be considered (the chief parts, those of George the Third and Queen Charlotte, had already been snapped up by Mrs Lace for herself and Noel). Actually all this was unnecessary. Jasper and Eugenia between them were getting on perfectly well with the arrangements, but it provided that for which Mrs Lace had been longing, namely, an excuse to show off to the neighbourhood her newly-acquired friends and lover.

It was, of course, rather annoying to her that she would be obliged to preserve Marjorie's incognito, and to refrain from whispered conjectures as to the identity of Noel; on the other hand, she considered that not even the assumed names of Foster and Jones entirely hid their intrinsic presentability, while Mr Aspect and Mrs St Julien were good fat fishes for her net. Besides, could she not look forward to that glorious day when she would be in the superior position of having 'known all along'? When Chalford learnt at last what greatness it had been harbouring in the shape of Noel, Chalford would see Mrs Lace in a dramatic light. People would be saying to each other: 'You remember, last summer. He was staying at the Jolly Roger and called himself Noel Foster, and that was when he fell in love with her. And now, only think of it, they have eloped together. Of course one always knew she wouldn't stay for long in this out-of-the-way place, the amazing thing is that she should ever have married such a dull bore —'

Even supposing that this dream of elopement which now filled her days should never come true, it would be known that Mrs Lace had been the love of Noel's life, and that although, for political or other reasons, he was unable to marry her, he still sent her a dried rose-leaf in a crested box once a year.

She decided that she would always thereafter dress herself in deepest mourning for her widowed heart. It would be wonderful, too, whispering to her intimates: 'I made him go back. He wished to give up all for me, but I could not allow that. He must have his career, do his duty, live his life. It is far better so. If I had allowed him to do as he wished he might have learnt in time to hate me; like this our love is fresh, eternal. No, my heart is broken, but I regret nothing.' Mrs Lace's imagination, which was vivid, ran away with her like this all the time.

The party was also intended to provide an opportunity of showing Noel that he was not the only pebble on Mrs Lace's beach; superfluous gesture, as poor Noel was already too firmly convinced that to see was to desire her. To this end the artistic Mr Leader and his colleagues were invited over from Rackenbridge, that local Athens which had, up to now, provided Anne-Marie with all her cultured conquests.

The great day dawned with thunder in the air, and soon after breakfast there was thunder in the Lace's drawing-room as well. Major Lace, filling up his pipe before setting out to examine a sick cow, remarked casually:

'Isn't it your binge today, Bella?'

Anne-Marie winced at this. She objected to the use of her real name, despised the word 'binge', and considered that Major Lace ought to have known as well as she did that it was *the* great day.

'I have asked a few people round at cocktail-time,' she said, in her society voice. 'Perhaps that's what you're thinking of?'

'Splendid! I thought it was today all right. I ran into old George

Wilkins yesterday at the Show, and told him to be sure and come along. Lucky thing I happened to remember about it. Why, he'll simply be the life and soul of a party like that.'

Anne-Marie froze on hearing this news. Then she flew into a passion. She refused to have Mr Wilkins at her party, he was quite unsuitable, an odious man, stupid and loutish. She hated him. She hated his red face, and Hubert knew that perfectly well, and Hubert had only asked him out of spite, in order to spoil everything for her. Everything. She burst into tears.

Major Lace listened to these recriminations with an expression of bewilderment which was by degrees succeeded by one of intense disgust on his kind round face.

'You're such a little snob, my dear,' he said, as soon as he was able to get a word in, 'I know what you're thinking, that those new grand friends of yours won't like poor old George Wilkins – eh? Well, as it happens you're wrong there, because I'm prepared to bet a large sum that they will. He's the most amusing fellow I've ever come across, and what's more, everybody likes old Wilkins – except you.'

'I'm not a snob,' cried Mrs Lace, angrily. 'If I were a snob should I be friends with penniless artists like Leslie Leader? On the contrary, many people would think I was too much the other way – not particular enough. It is not snobbish to demand certain qualities in one's acquaintances – and personally I prefer to mix with people of culture. I dislike vulgarity of mind. However, all this is beside the point. I shall be delighted for you to invite Mr Wilkins any other time. At this particular party it will be quite impossible to have him.'

'Why?'

'For the reasons I have given you. He is an unsuitable person, so *unsoigné* too. And for another thing, Leslie Leader would leave the house if he came. He absolutely hates him.'

'Dear, dear, does he now? Mr Leader goes up in my estimation. I never thought that white slug had the guts to hate anybody. Still I think I should risk it, rather awkward to put Leader off at the last minute like this.'

'Naturally there will be no question of doing that. I am going to ring up Mr Wilkins now this minute and tell him you have made a mistake.'

'Anne-Marie, you can do that if you like, but I warn you that I shan't turn up at your blasted party unless Wilkins does,' said Major Lace, setting his jaw.

'Nonsense, Hubert, of course you'll have to come. It would look very odd if you didn't, and besides, who's to mix the cocktails?'

'I don't give a damn who mixes the cocktails. Leader can mix them.'

'You know he can't; he's teetotal.'

'He would be. Anyway if I'm to come Wilkins must come, you can take it or leave it old girl.' So saying, Major Lace stumped off to his cow-byres.

Mrs Lace spent much of the morning in tears of rage. During luncheon she uttered no word, a fact which Major Lace apparently never noticed, as he went on as usual, chatting about John's disease, and the tubercular content of a pint of milk. He did not mention Mr Wilkins or the party, and the moment he had swallowed his food he went off again. Arrangements for the party occupied Anne-Marie's afternoon, but gave her little satisfaction. Even the arrival of Mr Leader, who came, as he had promised that he would, to decorate her drawing-room with whitewashed brambles and cellophane, failed to improve her temper.

While she was changing her dress, however, her spirits began to rise, and by the time that the first guests had appeared she became positively gay once more. She enjoyed entertaining more than anything else on earth, and was, considering her inexperience, a good enough hostess, unflagging in her zeal to please.

Neighbour after neighbour now arrived, husbands, wives, daughters, and an occasional son home on leave or down from Oxford. They were all jolly friendly, dull people, and were suitably startled by Anne-Marie's silver *lamé* cocktail-trousers and heavy make-up. The young men from Rackenbridge struck, she considered, exactly the right note of Bohemian négligé in their shrimp trousers and

'Aertex' shirts open at the neck. The scene, in fact, was now set for the entry of Mrs Lace's new friends. Anxiously she began to keep one eye on the drive, and for a whole hour she played Pagliacci, chatting and laughing with a breaking heart. For the new friends did not appear.

When finally they did turn up, fearfully late, and accompanied by a stockingless Eugenia, they all seemed to be in the last stages of exhaustion. 'We are quite worn out, you see,' Jasper explained politely, 'by Eugenia's party. It was an absolute riot from beginning to end. We think she is a genius Eugenia, Eugenius, E.U.G.E.N.I.A. Eugenia.'

'It was too lovely,' said Lady Marjorie, who appeared far less languid than usual. She had colour in her cheeks and her eyes shone. 'But why didn't you come, Mrs Lace; you can't imagine what a lovely party it was.'

'We sang Jackshirt hymns for hours outside the head-quarters,' said Poppy. '"Onward Union Jackshirts" – D'you know that one; shall we teach it you, another time perhaps? Then we went for a wonderful march with a band playing and we each carried a Union Jack. Marge and I have both joined up. The Comrades were heaven, so beautiful-looking.'

They all fell into chairs and fanned themselves. Poppy and Marjorie looked anything but smart London ladies, calculated to impress local housewives. Eugenia, her eye suddenly lighting upon Mr Leader pointed him out to Poppy, saying in a stage whisper, 'He's a well-known Pacifist. Shall we give him Union Jackshirt justice?'

'Not now,' Poppy whispered back, 'we're all much too tired.'

A sort of blight now began to fall on Mrs Lace's party. It was dreadful for her because nobody was behaving in the way she had planned they should. Most of the neighbours had gone home to their early dinners and those that remained formed little knots in the garden, talking to each other about sport or to Major Lace about the iniquities of the Milk Marketing Board. The Rackenbridge young men hung round the bar eating and drinking all they could lay their hands on, while her new friends were being in no way wonderful, but merely lay about the place in attitudes of extreme debility.

'We are so tired,' they reiterated apologetically, 'you should have seen what a distance we marched, it was terrible. In this heat too, whew!'

Poppy, who had a conscience about these things, did whisper in Jasper's ear that she thought they should mingle a bit more. Jasper replied, 'Mingle then,' but nothing happened.

Mrs Lace brought up Mr Leader and introduced him all round, saying, 'It was Leslie who did these wonderful decorations for me. He is a Surréaliste you know.'

Poppy said, politely, 'Oh! how interesting. Aren't you the people who like intestines and pulling out babies' eyes?'

Jasper said that he had once written a play, the whole action of which took place inside Jean Cocteau's stomach. 'Unfortunately I sold the film rights,' he added, 'otherwise you could have had them. The film was put on in Paris and many people had to leave the Jockey Club and stop being Roman Catholics because of it. I was pleased.'

Eugenia looked gloomily at Mr Leader, and said in a menacing voice, 'You should see the inside of the new Social Unionist head-quarters.'

'It's even more exciting than the inside of Jean Cocteau's stomach,' added Jasper.

After these sallies conversation died, and poor Mr Leader presently wandered away. Noel now lay back and put a newspaper over his face – nobody could have supposed, to see him, that he was madly in love with his hostess, nor were her guests at all likely to go home with the impression that between these two people was undying romance. Mrs Lace looked at him in despair.

Worse things, however, were to befall her. Presently the hated Mr Wilkins, looking even less *soigné* than usual, and covered with white dust, was shepherded into the room by Major Lace, who rubbed his hands together saying, 'Here's dear old George at last – broke down twice on the way! Still, better late than never, eh!

George? I thought that was your old bag of nails heard rattling up the drive. Cocktail or whisky and soda, eh?'

'I absolutely love that man's appearance,' Lady Marjorie whispered to Poppy.

'He certainly has a very whimsical face,' Poppy agreed.

At this juncture Mrs Lace was called away from the room to speak on the telephone. One of the neighbours had left a dust-coat behind and would call for it the following day. 'We loved your party,' she added. 'It was too bad we had to leave so early.' Mrs Lace agreed that it was too bad, promised to keep the dust-coat quite safely, and returned to the drawing-room, where an extremely painful sight met her eyes.

Mr Wilkins was seated on a sofa between Mrs St Julien and Lady Marjorie who were both doubled up with laughter. Mr Aspect, and the nameless but exalted Noel, crouching on the floor beside them, also appeared to be highly amused, whilst Major Lace stood over the whole group with the expression of a conjurer who has just produced from his sleeve some enchanting toy.

'And have you heard about the man who went into W. H. Smith?' Mr Wilkins was saying.

'No,' they cried, in chorus.

'He said to the girl behind the counter, "Do you keep stationery?" And she said, "No, I always wriggle."'

Roars of laughter greeted this story.

'And do you know about the man who was had up by the police?'

'No.'

'They said, "Anything you say will be held against you." He said, "*Anything* I say will be held against me?" and they said, "Yes," and he said, "Right oh, then, Greta Garbo."'

As Mrs Lace gazed with disgust upon this scene, she was approached by Mr Leader, who, looking as if he had a bad smell under his nose, came up to say goodbye.

'I will walk down the garden with you,' she said, glad of any excuse to take her away from hateful Mr Wilkins and his success.

'Dear, lovely Anne-Marie,' said Mr Leader, putting his hand on her arm, 'do explain your new friends to me – what is the point of them? You always used to tell me how much you dislike that sort of person, rich, smart, idle and stupid,' he spoke reproachfully.

'You don't quite understand,' said poor Mrs Lace. 'They are delightful really, only today they seem different. If you talked to them alone you wouldn't think them at all stupid.'

'My dear, they must be stupid if they have joined the Social Unionist party.'

'Oh! I think that's all a joke.'

'Social Unionism is no joke. It is a menace to the life's work of those who, like myself, love peace and wish all men equal. Surely, Anne-Marie, you cannot in two short weeks have forgotten all our wonderful ideals?'

'Oh! no,' said Anne-Marie, 'it's not that. But it is always interesting to meet new people, don't you think so, to try and get a view of life from their angle? And Noel Foster is, in many ways, very exceptional. The others are nice, but he is something different from what I have ever known. I can't explain why, you must meet him again, more quietly and see for yourself.'

'No thank you,' said Mr Leader, 'I have seen enough of him this afternoon.'

'I wondered,' Mrs Lace went on, 'whether all of you at Rackenbridge would help us with the pageant? We want various groups of people to undertake the different episodes, nothing is quite settled yet though.'

Mr Leader said he would think it over. 'I must say goodbye now, you wonderful creature. Don't forget that you are the greatest inspiration any man could have, and never waste your friendship on somebody who may be unworthy of such a gift.'

Mrs Lace could have kicked him for not making this pretty compliment in the hearing of Noel. She felt it to be utterly wasted among the dank laurels at the bottom of the garden.

When she got back to the house she found that all her guests had departed, with the exception of Mr Wilkins and his still admiring claque.

'Here's Anne-Marie,' said Noel, affectionately. 'Come over here and talk to us for a bit. You've been a hostess for long enough.'

'Oh! yes,' cried Poppy, making room for her on the sofa. 'We want you, we want to tell you all the things we've been fixing up for the pageant.'

'Ah! the pageant,' Mrs Lace felt happier. What mattered it that her cocktail-party had not been all she had hoped when she still had the pageant glowing on her horizon? She reminded herself that she and Noel were to play the parts of Queen Charlotte and George the Third. Together they would drive through cheering crowds, bowing to right and to left of them, a cynosure for all eyes, in the beautiful and historic coach that Lady Chalford was lending on that occasion.

This picture was constantly in Anne-Marie's mind; she thought about it nearly the whole time. How sweet and pretty she would look in her charming head-dress, how handsome the appearance of Noel in wig and uniform; how evident to all observers their great love for each other. In after days those who had seen them would be saying, 'What a pity we didn't know then who he really was. I suppose we might have guessed from the grace and ease with which he acknowledged the cheers. Of course, they were deeply in love, nobody could have failed to realize that. How romantic it all is!'

Perhaps their photograph would appear in the newspapers, a photograph in which Noel would be gazing at her, a whole wealth of love in his eyes. There was no end to the intoxicating vista of possibilities which stretched out before Anne-Marie when she began to think about the pageant.

What was Poppy saying now? 'Yes, it was Marge's idea. She is clever to have thought of it, and it's all quite settled. Mr Wilkins is going to be George the Third! He has promised he will at last, but we had to go down on our hands and knees to persuade him, didn't we, Mr Wilkins? And that will make the pageant a most wonderful success because no two people have ever looked so much alike as Mr Wilkins and George the Third; had you noticed it? Now you know we shall have to be getting back to Chalford because it's fearfully late and our dinner will be ready. We have loved the party, specially meeting Mr Wilkins. Thank you so much for it, and for introducing us to Mr Wilkins, it was heavenly of you. Goodbye Mr Wilkins, see you tomorrow then, at about one.'

Major Lace could not understand why his wife cried herself to sleep that night. He supposed that she must be in the family way again.

IO

Next day at the usual hour Noel pushed his way, hooting from time to time, through the undergrowth which surrounded his trysting-place. As he heard no answering cry, he presumed that Anne Marie had been unable to come. He found her lying, however, a little crumpled heap of despondency, on the steps of the temple, and very soon she was sobbing her heart out on Noel's shoulder.

'Darling, I really can't see that it matters as much as all that,' he said, when at last he had realized the reason for all this misery. 'Of course it would have been fun to do it together, and it is sweet of you to mind, but you know, Lady Marjorie is quite right, Mr Wilkins is the living double of George the Third. Rather clever of her to notice I thought.'

'Oh! you don't understand,' sobbed Mrs Lace. 'I'm not so stupid as to make all this fuss over an old pageant, although I had been looking forward to acting with you quite particularly.'

'Then what is it, my darling?' said Noel, who was getting rather bored with this scene.

'I'm so dreadfully, dreadfully unhappy.'

'Darling, why?'

'You're so unkind to me. I feel I can't bear it any longer.'

'Unkind?'

'All the secrecy.'

'What secrecy?'

Mrs Lace had now, more or less, recovered her composure. She knew that she looked pretty when she cried, so long as the crying only lasted a little while. Therefore, at the psychological moment she usually stopped. She did so now, and proceeded to comb her hair and powder her nose, peeping from beneath dewy eyelashes at Noel from time to time. There was an expression on his face which she interpreted as a warning not to go too far. In actual fact he was merely reminding himself that all women like an occasional good cry; it was a tax which lovers had to pay. He hoped that she would cut it short, meanwhile steeling himself to endurance.

'You see, darling,' she went on presently, 'it is rather cruel, the way you never tell me anything about yourself.'

Typical grievance, thought Noel. 'My darling,' he said, 'there really isn't much to tell. The history of my life up to date is extremely dull, believe me.'

'The smallest things about you are interesting to me,' said Anne-Marie, passionately.

'Well,' said Noel, with that bright facetiousness which was such an unattractive feature of his mind, 'shall we begin at the beginning? I was born of poor but honest parents —'

'Where?'

'Where was I born? I don't know exactly, it was somewhere in the Balkans. My father, you see, was an archaeologist, and he and my mother spent the first years of their married life wandering about in that part of the Continent. I know she had a bad time when I was born, as I was premature, and they could not get hold of a proper doctor for ages. They were both so vague, always.'

'Yes, I see. So then where were you educated?'

'In England, of course. After the War broke out circumstances compelled my parents to settle down at Hampton Court, and I went to a private school and to Eton in the ordinary way. They did want to send me to some foreign university, but there were various complications and in the end I went to Oxford.'

'And your parents – did they never go back?'

'No. After the War they said they were too old (they had married rather late in life). Besides, things had become so changed then, they preferred to stay on at Hampton Court. Now they are both dead.'

This conversation seemed to confirm suspicions which were

already forming in Mrs Lace's mind. Noel was obviously the rightful king of some Ruritania, preparing in the solitude of an English village for the *coup d'état* which should restore to him his throne. Any day now the courier might arrive and announce that the time was ripe, the people and the regiments in a proper frame of mind to welcome him back to the land of his fathers. Those two strange men whom she had noticed hanging about the Jolly Roger were doubtless members of his personal body-guard. Her total ignorance of central European politics and geography, coupled with an imaginative nature, enabled her to treat this conjecture as though it were a solid fact; she did not have the smallest misgiving about it from the first moment of its inception.

'What made you think of coming down here?' she asked, boldly.

Noel looked embarrassed. It would be difficult for him to explain his exact motives for coming to Chalford. He wondered whether Mrs Lace had spoken about this to Jasper, and if so what impression she had received from him. In order to be on the safe side, he muttered vaguely, 'Oh, I don't know, just waiting for something to turn up.'

The courier. The news from his Capital. 'And how long will it be before that happens? How much longer do you expect to be here?'

'Just as long as I can go on seeing you every day, darling Anne-Marie.'

'I wish you would take me away from here,' she cried, passionately.

Noel frowned. He had been anticipating some such development to this conversation. 'My dear,' he said, in a matter-of-fact voice, 'Whatever would your husband say if I did?'

'He would divorce me, and I shouldn't care a pin.'

'My darling Anne-Marie,' said Noel, kissing her hand and holding it in his, 'I must explain to you, I should have explained before – that I am not in a position to marry anybody. If I were, it would be my dream of dreams to marry you. But, for many reasons this is not possible, alas! You must take my word for it, dearest.'

Now for the storm, he thought, now for half an hour of hysterical reproaches. He knew exactly what would be said, he had heard it all before. 'To you I have been nothing except an agreeable summer holiday's diversion, but to me you are life itself,' and so on. It would take all his tact at the end of it to keep things on their old footing, as he very much hoped he would succeed in doing. For he still thought that Mrs Lace was a wildly attractive young woman.

There was a pause, during which he could feel the storm gathering. Metaphorically speaking, he cowered, putting up his coat collar. But to his enormous surprise and relief no storm broke. Mrs Lace encircled his neck with her arms and whispered in his ear, 'I quite understand, my own angel; don't let's think of this any more. We must be happy together whilst happiness is still possible, and try to forget that the day is at hand when we must part, perhaps for ever. And when that day does come, let us be brave and hide, from the world at any rate if not from each other, our broken hearts.'

Noel could hardly believe his ears. He thought that Mrs Lace was by far the most remarkable woman he had ever met.

'I always told you she was something out of the ordinary,' he said to Jasper that evening, after repeating the whole conversation for his benefit. They were on the best of terms now, Noel feeling so much gratitude for Jasper's surprisingly loyal intervention in this affair that he had forgiven and forgotten the piece of blackmail which had ensued. Ever since that afternoon when Jasper had been to see Anne-Marie she had shown a perfectly stupendous love for Noel, he felt that it would have taken weeks of diffident courtship on his part to produce such a result.

Jasper watched the situation developing itself with fiendish amusement, and could not resist telling Poppy what he had done.

'Oh! I say, poor Mrs Lace,' she said, laughing, 'anyway, I don't suppose she believed a word of it.'

'Didn't she just? Well then, why is she being so nice to Noel all of a sudden? She would hardly look at him before.'

'That's true. I think it's awfully funny, but awfully unkind of you, Jasper.'

'Not at all. The girl's having a fine time, and so is Noel. I think it was exceedingly nice of me, especially as I could have had her myself by raising a finger, and she's quite a cup of tea you know.'

'Really, Jasper, you are outrageous. Pass me the soap-dish, will you?'

Next time they were all together Poppy could not resist treating Noel with exaggerated deference for the benefit of Mrs Lace.

As for Anne-Marie, her dreams became daily more extravagant. She saw herself now as the central figure of an impending tragedy. The farewell scene – Noel booted and spurred, and glittering with decorations, kissing her goodbye in the moonlight while an equerry, holding two horses, awaited him at a discreet distance. 'Keep this ring and wear it always, it was my mother's.' He would tuck her little glove (or handkerchief, she had better order some new ones) into his belt, and gallop away, leaving her in a dead faint. Dreary weeks would follow, during which she would scan the papers for news of his triumph. Then, much later on, the wedding. Anne-Marie, drawn as by a magnet to his capital, would be standing in the crowd while Noel rode in state to marry some royal princess of an unexampled hideosity. His eye would light upon her as she stood there heavily veiled, and pierce her disguise. He would turn deathly pale and bite his lip until the blood came, to hide its quivering. Then, regaining his composure with a kingly gesture, he would ride on amid the huzzas of the populace. At that moment the assassin would draw his weapon, quick as thought she would throw herself before him, and stop the bullet with her own body, to die a few minutes later in the arms of Noel. As he closed her eyes he would pluck from his bosom, and pin to hers, the highest Order that was his to bestow. An alternative. Perhaps in the hour of his triumph he would send for her and install her in some gorgeous palace, joined to his own by an underground tunnel. She would be his good genius, guiding him with her wonderful feminine intuition through the quagmire of internal and international politics. The statesmen of all countries would bow before her and solicit her good offices with the king, and when she died her strange life would be written in several different languages. In fact, there was no end to these interesting possibilities.

The day after his scene with Mrs Lace, Noel was obliged to go to London. His lawyer wanted to see him; a visit to his dentist was becoming necessary. Jasper suggested that as he was going anyway, he should use the opportunity to buy some little present for Anne-Marie.

'I've never known it do much harm at this stage in the proceedings,' he said, 'and after all, you're simply stiff with cash old boy aren't you?'

Noel said it was no thanks to Jasper if he was. He thought the idea a good one, however, and when he had finished all his business and eaten his luncheon he went to a pawnshop and bought a small but pretty aquamarine set in a ring. The price, as the jeweller told him, was extremely reasonable, and this was because the market had been flooded ever since the sale of the Russian Imperial jewels, which had included several parures of this stone.

When he slipped his present on to Anne-Marie's finger he said, to make it seem more romantic, 'This ring, my beloved, once shone upon the finger of an Empress, but she wasn't half as beautiful as you.'

'An Empress!' cried Mrs Lace. 'How wonderful!'

Meanwhile arrangements for the pageant were going ahead in good earnest. It had been settled that the inhabitants of the Jolly Roger, Mrs Lace, Eugenia and her Comrades of the Chalford Branch, were to be responsible between them for providing all the clothes and for the opening scene, in which George the Third would arrive and be welcomed to Chalford House. After this, George and Charlotte, surrounded by their courtiers, were to mount a small platform on which there would await them two thrones, and here they would remain whilst the other scenes, consisting of salient events of the reign, were enacted on the lawn before them. These episodes were being entrusted by Eugenia to various neighbouring branches of Social Unionists, each branch to be responsible for one episode. (Mr Leader and his friends, having learnt that the pageant was in aid of the Social Unionist funds, had politely intimated to Mrs Lace that they would be unable to help.)

Rehearsals for the first scene had already begun. Mrs Lace, having resigned herself to the dismal necessity of driving with Mr Wilkins, was greatly cheered when Jasper promised her that Noel, taking the part, and wearing the actual clothes of the Lord Chalford of the day, should receive them at the front door, help her from the coach and arm her to the platform, where he would then present an address of welcome. Eugenia, as the Prince of Wales, Poppy as Fanny Burney, and Lady Marjorie as the Duchess of Devonshire, would also be there to greet them with billowing curtsies. Mrs Lace felt that after all there would now be even greater opportunities for interplay of flirtatious gestures between herself and Noel than if they had arrived together in the coach, and was happy. Jasper, when the first rehearsal was over, told Poppy that in the minds of those who saw the pageant horrid scandals would be associated with the hitherto unsullied name of Queen Charlotte.

Lady Chalford had invited Jasper to write and produce the pageant on the grounds of his grandfather's well-remembered talent for composing Valentines. Jasper was finding the job anything but agreeable, each decision in turn seemed to give offence to somebody, while Eugenia plagued him unmercifully, insisting that he must introduce a strong Social Unionist interest.

'My dear child, I don't see how I can,' he said, in despair. 'I mean, think for yourself, what have George the Third and Social Unionism in common? Not one single thing.'

'And what about the Glory of England?' cried Eugenia, in a grandiose voice.

'Glory of bottoms. The ordinary person simply remembers George the Third by the fact that he went mad and lost America. That's all he's ever supposed to have done for England, poor old boy.'

'I can't help it,' said Eugenia, 'If we are having a Grand Social Unionist rally and pageant, Social Unionism has got to come into it somehow.'

Jasper tore his hair.

Next day Eugenia appeared very early at the Jolly Roger having spent a sleepless night in the throes of composition. As soon as Jasper was up she handed him a document, which ran as follows:

SPEECH BY GEORGE THE THIRD

Hail! and thanks for all your good wishes, we are happy to be among our loyal Aryan subjects of Chalford and district. In our speech today we thought we would tell you of a very curious prophetic dream which we had last night. We dreamt that by degrees this, our glorious country, will begin to sink into the slush and slime of a decaying democracy. America, as we are sure you must have all noticed with horror, is already tainted with the disease, and we expect we shall soon have to be kicking her out of our glorious Empire; but even this wonderfully foreseeing action on our part won't make any difference in the long run. Nothing can save our country from a contagion which is to sweep the earth. Never mind, Britons, do not despair, for in our dream we foresaw that when you shall have been plunged into the darkest night, governed (if one can use such a word) by a pack of disastrous old ladies who ought to have been dead for years, a new day will dawn, the old ladies will be forced to retire to their unhallowed beds, and their place at Westminster will be taken by young and victorious Comrades. In those days, the streets will ring with the cry of youths who will march, each carrying his little banner, towards the fulfilment of a Glorious Britain. A new spirit, the spirit of Social Unionism will be abroad in the land, vitality will flow back into her withered veins, hateful democracy will die the death. We will now all sing the Social Unionist Hymn, 'Land of Union Jackshirts, Mother of the Flag.'

'What d'you think of it?' asked Eugenia, anxiously.

'It's a fine speech,' said Jasper, who had evidently got some beer up his nose and was choking into a handkerchief.

When Mr Wilkins saw it he said that it was very good but much too long for him to learn by heart.

'Oh! you must try,' said Eugenia. 'It would spoil a speech like that if you read it. Learn one sentence every day – you've got heaps of time.'

'I'll try,' said Mr Wilkins, good-naturedly.

'I'm hoping,' continued Eugenia, 'that you will join the Social Unionist party. You are asked to pay ninepence a month, the Union Jack shirt costs five shillings and the little emblem sixpence. When you have signed on you will be able to use the head-quarters as much as you like. I hope to arrange for instruction in boxing and other Social Unionist sports there soon, and we shall be having a social every Tuesday evening as well. So do join up.'

'Anything to please you, Miss Eugenia, but I'm afraid I don't know much about it at present. Wait a minute, though, is it against foreigners and the League of Nations, because if so I'll join with pleasure. Damned sewers.'

Mr Wilkins had spent several years tea-planting in Ceylon where 'sewer' is apparently a usual term of approbrium.

'It is,' said Eugenia, earnestly. 'Some of us think of sterilizing all foreigners, you know, but I'm not sure our Captain would go quite as far as that.'

'That's the stuff to feed the troops! Well done! just what they need. I think Hitler's a splendid fellow too, although I'm not sure he doesn't carry things a shade far sometimes. I mean, shoot up the chaps as much as you like, but don't kill their wives at breakfast – Eh?'

'When shooting is in progress,' said Eugenia, coldly, 'the woman's duty is to retire to her proper place, the bedroom. If she interferes in men's business she must put up with a man's fate.'

'There's something in what you say, by Jove; women are a damned sight too fond of poking their noses into things that are none of their business, these days specially. Look here, I'm joining up; what did you say I owe you?'

'Ninepence a month, the Union Jack shirt costs five shillings, and sixpence for the little emblem. You sign here – see?'

Jasper's embarrassment as pageant producer reached a climax when Poppy came to him and said, 'Look here, darling, Marge wants to know whether she can't be Queen Charlotte instead of Mrs Lace. Do say "Yes".'

'No, really, I don't think she can,' said Jasper, 'and anyway why does she want to be, all of a sudden like this?'

'Well, she didn't want me to tell you, but I suppose I shall have to. The fact is, you see, she's keen on Mr Wilkins, and so of course she quite naturally wants to drive in the coach with him.'

'Darling Miss Smith, you'll have to tell her to be sensible. Tell her she can make eyes at him on the platform as much as she likes (she had better take a lesson in amorous gestures from Mrs Lace), but I don't see how the whole works can be altered now.'

'Oh, dear! Oh, dear! Marge will be simply furious. She is used to getting her own way in life.'

'All I can say is that she must be furious for once. Why, it's as much as my place is worth to tell Mrs Lace she can't be Queen Charlotte – Noel would stop paying my expenses down here most likely, if I did, and you don't want me to go straight back to London, I suppose! No, my angel, I'm sorry but it's quite out of the question. Tell you what I will do though, if you like.'

'What's that?'

'I'll give you a good bite on the back of your neck.'

'No, thank you,' said Poppy, 'I'm a mass of bruises as it is.'

The question, however, was by no means dropped, Lady Marjorie herself coming to the charge, hotly supported by Eugenia.

'Is this to be a Great Social Unionist rally, or not?' the latter demanded furiously, 'because if it is, it stands to reason that we must keep the best parts for Union Jackshirts. Mrs Lace is not only

90

not one of us, she is a well-known friend of Pacifists – in fact, it would never surprise me if she should turn out to be a Pacifist spy. How absurd then to insist that she shall be the one to drive along hailed by Social Unionist cheers.'

'I dare say, but you should have thought of all this sooner,' said Jasper, with some irritation, 'before it was settled. Personally, I don't give a damn who plays which part, and I wish you were all at the bottom of the sea, anyway, but you might remember that wretched old Local Beauty is slaving herself to death over your dresses, and if she wants to take the part of the least attractive queen in history, I should have thought it would be a matter of ordinary decency to let her. In any case you must arrange it among yourselves, I absolutely refuse to make any such suggestion to her.'

'Oh, well, I see your point,' said Lady Marjorie, good-temperedly, 'I'll ask her myself at the committee meeting tomorrow.'

Mrs Lace, however, when approached was perfectly firm. She listened calmly while the suggestion was being made, and then said that it was too unlucky, but Queen Charlotte's dress was now finished, and could never be altered to fit Lady Marjorie, as there were no means of letting out the seams on the hips and round the waist. Marjorie, who had never been spoken to in such a way before, was more surprised than angry, and took her defeat with the greatest of good humour. Poppy and Eugenia were furious, and said afterwards that Mrs Lace was a spiteful cat, and Poppy said at the time to Mrs Lace that as she looked exactly like Queen Charlotte, she was quite right to keep the part. Unfortunately, owing to its target's total ignorance of English history, this Parthian shaft went wide of the mark.

Noel and Jasper, who seldom met these days, over a quiet glass at the Rose Revived, made a point of doing so now, and agreed together that women were impossible everywhere, except in what Eugenia had referred to as their proper place. Noel no longer took Mrs Lace's side on every subject; feeling quite certain, as he now did, of her great love for him, he was able to adopt a high-handed attitude towards her, and was by no means inclined to jeopardize all future relations with Eugenia Malmains on her account.

Mrs Lace, on her part, secure in the knowledge of her own romantic situation, felt that she could now alienate dukes' ex-fiancées and earls' granddaughters with the most perfect indifference. She carried her head in the air and permitted herself the luxury of being extremely disagreeable to everybody except Noel.

II

Meanwhile the two detectives continued to ply their lugubrious trade. They appeared to ignore the necessity for repose, and the inhabitants of the Jolly Roger were continually being startled by their appearance in the most unexpected places. They would jump out from dark corners like sinister Jack-in-the-Boxes, at all times of the day and night. It was most unnerving. Finally, Jasper made a heroic if unsuccessful attempt to win their confidence. He stood them drink after drink at the bar. Their heads proved to be of the ox-like variety; and although they unbent after the fourth whisky sufficiently to admit to their profession, and made after the seventh some startling disclosures as to the present tendencies of modern London society, human ingenuity and liberality could push them no further than this. The two things which Poppy was so anxious to find out, namely, whether Anthony St Julien himself was employing them or whether it was the mother of his débutante, and how much or how little they knew of her relationship with Jasper, remained locked in their own bosoms. The end of the matter was that the detectives were obliged to carry Jasper upstairs to bed, where he lay, fully clothed and staring at the electric light bulb until far on into the next day.

'Never mind,' he said to Poppy, when he had more or less recovered from the attack of alcoholic poisoning which ensued, 'I am on exceedingly good terms with them now, which is always something. The worst of it is that I rather think I told them about us being engaged. Would that matter, do you suppose?'

'I don't know,' said Poppy. 'I don't think it was very clever of you and anyway we're not.'

'Oh! aren't we? I thought we were?'

'Not at all,' said Poppy. 'You might bear in mind the fact that I have a perfectly good husband already, would you?'

'Perfectly good strikes me as an euphemism. Besides, it's quite obvious to any thinking man that you are heading for the divorce courts at present.'

'That's no reason for wanting to marry you,' said Poppy, 'and anyway I hope you always take very good care to come in through Marge's room. You do, now don't you, Jasper?'

'I do when I remember. That sort of thing is so awfully easy to forget.'

'I'd be very much obliged if you would bear it in mind all the same. After all, I've only got to hold out for long enough and Anthony St. Julien will be forced to let me divorce him. Then we shall be on clover.'

'Only so-so. Remember what awful times the innocent party has before the absolute, with the King's Proctor breathing down its neck every night. I often think one should look at every side of a question before settling upon a course of action. However, I see you are admitting our engagement; that's always something.'

'Indeed. I am not.'

'Now I have thought out a very good scheme whereby we might yet be able to raise some money to live on. We will go and see my grandfather, who is binned-up in an asylum near here. He may fall for you (it seems to run in the family), and come across with the goods. You never know.'

'If he's binned-up he won't have any goods to come across with, will he?' said Poppy.

'That's just where you're wrong, little Miss Know-all. You see, my grandfather is in a very special kind of bin, for lunatic peers only, and it has quite different rules from the ordinary sort. It was endowed by some rich old peeress in 1865 who was clearly insane herself; she had it built on the exact plans of the House of Lords, so that the boys should feel at home, and she made up the rules as she went along. I once got hold of a copy of them, feeling it might come in handy – here we are.' He pulled a bundle of typescript out of his pocket. 'I'll read you out the bits that matter,' he said. 'First of all there's a sort of preface, pointing out that madness is an infliction which can befall any one of us, from the most humble to the most noble, and that therefore it is quite possible even for peers of the realm to be attacked by this distressing malady. The old girl goes on to say that for too long it has been a disgraceful scandal, a blot on the name of England, that such quantities of these poor, good old men should, through no fault of their own, have been allowed to perish in the hateful and unrefined atmosphere of the common mad-house. This scandal apparently weighed on her mind to such a degree that she spent most of her time visiting the poor good old men and trying to ease their lot by reading to them, teaching them poker work and other useful and profitable occupations, and providing them, as far as the regulations of their bins permitted, with those little luxuries which do so much to make life worth living. "I feel," she says, "and our dear Queen has been gracious enough to approve of my sentiments on this subject, that the *most* one can do for gentlemen who have so *faithfully* served their Sovereign and their Country, but who through the inscrutable visitation of Providence have been rendered unable, not only to continue such service, but to enjoy any of the amenities of life, and worse yet are cut off from the society of their *loved* ones and of those of their fellow peers upon whom the infliction has *not yet* fallen, can never be too much." And so on and so forth. Now – are you listening, Miss Smith – here is the rule on which I build my hopes, Rule 6.

'"In order that these unhappy noblemen should be enabled to preserve that measure of self-respect which their birth should guarantee, but of which circumstances too often conspire to rob them, the inhabitants of Peersmont shall be entitled, under this foundation, to the full and entire control of one half of their incomes during life; and to the full and entire disposal, by testament, of one half of their fortune after death."

'That's quite plain, isn't it? You see she made up all these rules for the place and they were ratified by Act of Parliament. Now I happen to know that the old boy, my grandfather, is worth over a million altogether, and he is a complete miser, so it stands to reason that if he has been controlling, say £25,000 a year for the thirty years that he has spent at Peersmont, he must now be worth a tidy penny. On the other hand, it is like squeezing blood out of a stone to get any of it. I know my poor mother has been going to see him for years and has never managed to extract a penny. Uncle Bradenham is a miser too, it's a family trait.'

'Doesn't sound all that hopeful,' said Poppy.

'It's pretty hopeless I can tell you, that's why I've never bothered to go and see the old boy before. All the same, there can be no harm in trying, and it would be quite funny to see over Peersmont. Lady Chalford keeps on offering to lend me her car whenever I want it, so I vote we go over there one day this week and try our luck, eh?'

'K.O.,' said Poppy indifferently.

Jasper went to see Lady Chalford about the pageant, as indeed he did most days, and asked whether he could borrow the car. They were on very good terms; she thought him a delightful young man, and made no secret of her wish that he should ally himself to her family by marrying Eugenia; Jasper, on his side, was getting very much attached to the old lady.

'By all means,' she said, 'I shall be enchanted to lend you the car. Yes, take Poppy with you; it will do poor Driburgh good to see her pretty face. Now which day had you thought of going? Tomorrow? Very well then, I shall tell the gardener that he is to pick a really first-class bunch of grapes and some peaches for you to give dear Driburgh from me with very many messages. I shall be very anxious to have an account of how you find him.'

Jasper was pleased to hear this. First-class grapes and peaches were a long-felt want at the Jolly Roger, where the strawberries were over and the raspberries were becoming decidedly squashy.

'Should he seem to be more or less himself,' Lady Chalford continued, little suspecting that such black thoughts lurked in the mind of her young friend, 'my dear husband and I would be most happy to receive him here some time. Now I wonder, for instance, if the curator would permit him to come over to see the pageant. Anyhow, I leave it in your hands, Mr Aspect, to do as you think best.'

Lady Chalford then spoke of the pageant. 'You have all been most kind. I am more grateful to you than I can say for relieving me of any trouble in this matter. It would have been far beyond my powers to organize a thing of this sort, living as I have for so long in seclusion. That dear little woman, Mrs Lace now – so clever of you to find her. She tells me that she knows all the neighbours for miles around. I have asked her to revise my list so that we can send out the invitations. My husband's agent will then look through it for me and tell me all about the people, so that I can be quite sure that I shall ask nobody who it would be unsuitable for my little Eugenia to meet. One cannot be too careful, of course. Mrs Lace herself is, he tells me, the daughter of a rural dean, and Lace I know to be a much-respected name in these parts; the family has lived at Comberry for a hundred years or more and Major Lace is a lay rector. I am perfectly contented for Eugenia to make friends with them, quite suitable people. Now, tell me, when is dear Poppy's husband expected down here?'

12

Poppy and Jasper bowled across the sixteen odd miles of rural England which lay between Chalford and Peersmont in an ancient maroon-coloured Rolls-Royce, the one concession made by Lord and Lady Chalford to the age of progress. Instead of being carried along in an almost recumbent position, seeing nothing except gleaming paint-work, as in modern cars, they sat bolt upright and enjoyed a full view of the summer landscape. The inside of the car smelt rather musty and the upholstery was hidden under holland covers.

The countryside looked extremely beautiful, covered as it was with alternate acres of golden corn, dark-green woods and lemon-coloured stubble dotted with stooks of corn. The heat was intense. Poppy said how sad it made her feel when she thought that in a very few years time these lovely lonely stretches would probably be covered with mean little jerry-built houses.

'Think of Sussex,' she said with a shiver, 'how agreeable it would be if England could become much poorer, smaller, inconspicuous among nations and civilized once more.'

'Becoming poorer won't necessarily make her more civilized,' said Jasper. 'Civilization is dependent on one economic factor and that is extreme inequalities of wealth. The inevitable advent of Socialism, whether national or international, will be the fatal blow to what is left of our civilization.'

'If that is your view I am surprised that you should have joined Eugenia's party, which is obviously a form of national Socialism, isn't it?'

'I prefer national Socialism to the other sort, it is so much more romantic. Besides, I am inclined to think that the Western civilization we know needs putting out of its agony as soon as possible.

It is old and tired, the dark ages are practically upon us anyhow, and I should prefer that they march in with trumpet and flag than that they should creep upon us to the tap of the typewriter. I am at heart, I suppose, a Nihilist.'

'I don't know what that is,' said Poppy.

'No! But then you are a girl with a very limited outlook, aren't you?'

'I'm not.'

'Oh! yes, you are. Like most women you only care about personalities, things don't interest you.'

'That's simply not true. I'm fearfully interested in things – I absolutely long for a sable coat.'

'Don't be flippant, it irritates me.'

'Well, it's a fact,' said Poppy, defiantly, 'and I should be quite happy for ever if I had one.'

'Really! women are extraordinary.'

'All the same darling, you do love me, don't you?'

'I'm bound to say I do. But I should love you a great deal more if you were my intellectual equal.'

'As I'm always telling you – you ought to marry Marge. She speaks four languages.'

'As I'm always telling you, there's nothing would suit me better, but you're so idle, you never take any kind of steps to arrange it for me.'

'Too late now, she's nuts about Mr Wilkins – simply nuts. You can't imagine how she dotes on that man.'

'More than you dote on me?'

'Much more. He's literally the only chap she has ever been keen on you see, so she thinks him perfect. She has nothing else to compare him with.'

'I'm bound to say it has made a great difference to her. She is quite civil to me now instead of biting my head off whenever I speak as she did at first. Love is an exceedingly remarkable thing, in some ways. So what is she going to do about it?'

'Well, I believe she has written to Osborne to tell him definitely that their engagement is off – she was keeping him on a string before, like Nellie Bly and the fly you know. I say, look at that little white house. I wouldn't mind living there, would you?'

'And what are her intentions towards Mr Wilkins?'

'Strictly honourable. She's decided to wait a fortnight, and then propose to him if he hasn't done anything about it by then. I'm sure he won't have, he's obviously a man of no imagination or initiative.'

'Of course she's an exceedingly horizontal girl,' said Jasper in a contemplative voice. 'All the same, I should say that Mr Wilkins is a lucky chap.'

'Oh! he is indeed.'

'What's she worth?'

'She's fabulously rich. Her father left something like three millions, I believe.'

'Makes me sick,' said Jasper, 'you see that definitely shows I must be a Nihilist, otherwise why should I be engaged to the only poor girl in the parish.'

'You're not engaged. And there's still Eugenia,' said Poppy.

'Eugenia's a fine girl, but it's you I'm in love with, darling Miss Smith.'

'Good,' said Poppy, bouncing over to his side of the car and putting her arm round his waist. 'Hullo! there's something hard and bulging in your pocket – what is it?'

'I had an idea that, as we are unlikely to get anything out of my old man, it might be a good plan to translate this visit into terms of hard cash at the earliest opportunity. There's a chap on the *Evening Banner* who will give me £50 for a photograph of grand-father – you see they've only got one of him taken seventy years ago in his Fauntleroys and as he's bound to die soon they'll be needing a more recent one for the obituary. So I brought this "Kodak" along (they are very strictly forbidden in Peersmont). I found it in Mrs Lace's house the first time I went there and thought it might come in handy.'

When they arrived at Peersmont village they stopped at a

public-house and had what Poppy described afterwards as a fairly delicious but really rather disgusting lunch, over which they sat for such an immoderate length of time that it was already past four o'clock when they set forth, again in the Rolls-Royce, for the asylum. They drove through a grim Victorian medieval gateway flanked on either side by huge black walls, on the top of which were a double row of revolving spikes. Inside, the grounds were dank with conifers, in the midst of which there suddenly appeared the towers and spires of the Houses of Parliament, looking strangely uncomfortable in their rustic setting. The chauffeur drew up without any hesitation at the Peers' entrance, when the door of the car was immediately flung open by a policeman, who asked their business.

'The Duke of Driburgh?' said Jasper casually.

'I believe His Grace is in the House at present,' replied the policeman, 'would you kindly step this way and I will tell the curator that you are here. What name, please?'

He led them across the courtyard towards what should have been the House of Commons but which was, it appeared, the residential part of the asylum. The curator sat in a little Gothic room tremendously decorated with wood carvings, and received them warmly. He was a charming young man.

'The Duke of Driburgh?' he said, when Jasper had explained who he was. 'Splendid! The duke will be most awfully pleased to see you, I know. But look here, the House is sitting at the moment, can you wait until it rises? It won't be more than another half-hour at the outside, there is very little business today. In fact I would send for him at once except that he happens to be deputizing for our Lord Chancellor, Lord Rousham, who is on the sick-list again – no, nothing at all serious I am glad to say. He has just nipped up to the top of a big elm tree and is building himself a nest there. We don't stop him nowadays, one is never supposed to stop them doing harmless things of that sort. He won't catch a chill in this warm weather and the others like to watch how the nest is getting along. Rather fun for them really.'

'How interesting,' said Jasper. 'And has my grandfather any little hobbies of that sort?'

'Nothing in the least spectacular. He is fond of building and reads a great deal of Rider Haggard. A few bricks and a bucket of white paint keep him happy for hours, he thinks the paint is mortar you see. But he has never had an outburst since he came here, he is very easy from my point of view.'

'What was he shut up for?' said Jasper, 'I have often wondered, but it happened years before I was born, and has been kept very dark in the family ever since.'

'I'm not absolutely certain myself – I could look it up in the records for you though. Let me see' – he opened a drawer and took out of it a card-index – 'A.B.C.D. Driburgh. Here we are. Oh, yes, of course, I remember now. He was shooting over his estate and something annoyed him – the birds were going in the wrong direction or something like that. Anyway the result was that he deliberately shot a gamekeeper and three beaters straight off, two left and rights. Curious little nerve storm, he always seems quite sane here. A very leading figure in the political line, you know.'

'And what are his political opinions?' asked Poppy with a slight giggle, which was hastily checked as the curator gave her a severe look. She gathered that jokes about the inmates and their eccentricities were not much encouraged.

'The duke is an out-and-out Tory and anti-White Paper man.'

'But I imagine they are all that?' said Jasper.

'My dear sir, you are very much mistaken. We have comparatively few reactionary peers, the majority here are moderate Baldwinites; among the Liberals there are some extremely advanced thinkers, and besides that we can boast no fewer than four Communists and two Scottish Nationalists.'

An electric bell now rang twice on the curator's table.

'House up,' he said, 'even sooner than I had expected. Come along with me will you and I'll find the duke for you. By the way, that object in your pocket – it's not a camera, is it?'

'No indeed,' said Jasper, 'I am more than a little deaf and it is an instrument to assist my hearing.'

The curator blushed. 'I am so sorry,' he said. 'I was obliged to ask you, as cameras are most strictly forbidden here.'

'Naturally,' said Jasper.

The curator now led them out on to the terrace which, like its prototype at Westminster, overhung a sheet of water and was covered with dainty tea-tables. Trooping on to it from another entrance was a throng of funereal-looking and for the most part ancient gentlemen. As they emerged some of them formed little groups animated with earnest conversation, while others made straight for the tea-tables, loudly ordering vanilla ices, crumpets, raspberry jam or sausages and mash.

'Ah! Duke,' said the curator. Breaking into one of the groups he buttonholed a tall, rather paunchy but handsome old man and conducted him towards the place where Jasper and Poppy stood waiting. 'Here are two visitors to see you, your grandson Mr Aspect, and Mrs St Julien.'

'My boy,' said the duke, in tones of exaggerated emotion. His watery eyes brimmed over and a large tear splashed the pavement. He took hold of Jasper's arm in two places and shook it up and down with vigour. 'My boy. Very good of you to come and see your old grandfather. Not many of my descendants can be bothered to these days.'

The curator slipped away.

The duke then greeted Poppy with a courtly bow and conducted them both to an adjacent table. When they were seated Jasper said, 'My *fiancée*,' indicating Poppy.

'Yes, yes, I suppose so,' said the duke. 'Charming little lady. I always used to think, in my younger days, that it takes a lot to beat a pretty widow, and you are a very pretty widow my dear, if I may be permitted to say so.' He pressed his foot gently on Poppy's underneath the table. She gave him an inviting smile, whereupon he proceeded to hold her hand as well. 'And when are you going to be married may I ask – lucky fella,' he said, turning towards Jasper, but firmly retaining Poppy's hand.

'That's just what we wanted to discuss with you sir,' said Jasper, 'because we would do nothing without your approval naturally. As soon as Mrs St Julien consented to become my wife I said we must come over and ask for your blessing. We are staying at Chalford you see.'

'Upon my soul, that was very polite and considerate of you, young man,' cried the duke heartily. 'Not one of my own children ever bothered about a thing like that, I'm most extremely touched. Charming little lady too, charming. So what are you up to these days, Jasper my boy – soldier, sailor, candle-stick maker, or what, eh?'

'Well, at the moment I'm out of work,' said Jasper. 'A gentleman of leisure you might say.' He was not very sure how this news would be received. Other elderly persons of his acquaintance were always trying to chivvy him into jobs of extraordinary uncongeniality. He need have had no qualms, the duke was delighted.

'That's damned good news, by Jove,' he said, 'damned good. Why I do believe you're the only one of my grandsons who is not in trade. I hate trade, it's not suitable for a gentleman. Gentlemen, my grandsons, should have leisure and plenty of it, I hate all this hurrying about, getting up early in the morning to sell motor cars and such nonsense. Bradenham's sons all do it, most inconsiderate of them, in my opinion. It lets down the traditions of of a fine old family. Gentlemen should go into politics, that's their duty – to govern the country, it's the only thing they're fit for anyway.

'What are your politics, my boy?'

'I'm an out-and-out anti-White Paper Tory,' said Jasper advisedly.

'Splendid. I can see that we shall get on famously. And you don't stand for Parliament?'

'I can't afford to,' said Jasper, who was longing to bring the conversation round to the subject of money.

'Quite right. Nobody can afford to get mixed up with that rabble in the Commons, it's the greatest mistake, believe me. If you wait long enough they're bound to give you a peerage, always do in the end, and then you'll be able to come here. This is the only legislative assembly that's worth two pins these days, I assure you.'

There was a silence, while Jasper racked his brains to think of the most pleasing terms in which a request for money could be couched. The duke, however, relieved him of the necessity by saying, 'Only wish I could do something for you, my boy, pay off your debts or make you an allowance, but there it is – I hope you understand the situation. I expect I am poorer than you are, if anything.'

Jasper looked at Poppy and raised his eyes to heaven.

'We landowners,' continued the duke, 'are very hard hit in these days. Ever since finance bills have been taken out of our hands, in the Lords, the country has gone from bad to worse. We have had one Socialist government after another, I don't know which are more Socialistic, the Labour people or these milk-and-water White-Paper, lily-livered, black-hearted, so-called Conservatives. It's a scandal. They take half your income away before you have a chance of getting at it, and the other half shortly afterwards. Hard times for millionaires these are, I can tell you. Then you know my expenses here' (he lowered his voice) 'are very heavy – very. Why, a pot of tea costs sixpence and I must say I do like to have a crumpet with it sometimes – fourpence! Rank profiteering of course. However, tell you what I'll do, my boy. I'll send up to my bank and find out if I haven't got some little trinket there that this charming lady would accept as a wedding present.'

'Oh! thank you so much, you are kind,' said Poppy sweetly. Jasper, envisaging a seed-pearl locket, merely scowled.

At this moment a slight commotion broke out the other side of the terrace. Two liveried attendants sprang forward and led away between them a young man of untidy appearance who was gesticulating wildly. The other peers seemed totally uninterested by this occurrence.

'That's Gunnersbury,' said the duke, 'dreadful fellow. A shocking Socialist you know.'

'Poor thing, he seems to be in a great stew,' said Poppy.

'All the Labour peers are very much upset at the moment, it's about a bill of theirs we flung out last week. They called it the Toll of the Roads or some such nonsense and they kept us up until four o'clock one morning talking the most utter gibberish you can possibly imagine. It appears that every year a few thousand totally unimportant persons are killed on the roads, and that lunatic Gunnersbury, supported by some squeamish asses on the Labour benches, brought in a bill to abolish all motor transport. These Socialists put a perfectly exaggerated value on human life, you know. Ridiculous. As I said in my speech, what on earth does it matter if a few people are killed, we're not at war are we? We don't need 'em for cannon fodder? Then what earthly good do they do to anybody? Kill 'em on the roads by all means, they come off the unemployment figures and nobody is likely to be any the wiser.'

'I see your point,' said Jasper. 'So I suppose you had a fairly heated debate?'

'Very heated indeed. However, we Tories won the day – we always do, of course, there's some sense talked in this place let me tell you. All the same, these Labour fellows are a perfect curse, for ever bringing in some ludicrous bill or other, and then making the dickens of a fuss because they are in the minority here. Damned good thing for the country if they are, I should say. That blasted fool Lord Williams now, red-hot Communist if you please, brought in a bill the other day to try and substitute dandelions for strawberry leaves on our coronets and rabbit skins for ermine on our robes. Anybody would think the poor chap wasn't quite right in the head, the way he goes on.'

The duke then took them for a short stroll in the park, which was dank and gloomy. During the course of it, however, Jasper managed to obtain several promising snapshots of his grandfather as well as an interesting study of Lord Rousham, who, peeping over the edge of his nest as they passed, began to pelt them with orange-peel, chattering wildly to himself.

'Wonderful fellow, Rousham,' said the duke, hardly bothering even to look up, 'he can turn his hand to anything, you know. That's a first-class nest he has made. They tell me it is entirely lined with pieces of the India Report. Of course we miss him in the House just now, but I bet you he is doing good work up there all the same.'

Presently they were joined by the curator, who had come to inform Jasper that all visitors must be outside the park by six o'clock.

'That'll be in ten minutes time,' he said. 'Why don't you come again and take the duke out? We always allow it in the case of the moderate ones. There is an excellent tuckshop in the village and they love to go there, it makes a nice change for them.'

'I'll do that one day,' said Jasper. 'I had thought of taking him over to see Lady Chalford as I know she would be pleased. And by the way, there is to be a garden party and pageant at Chalford House next Wednesday week, and she asked me to find out whether you would care to come over for it, and bring any of the peers with you?'

The curator accepted this invitation with pleasure, and so, when it was put to him, did the Duke of Driburgh. After this, Poppy and Jasper, feeling more exhausted than if they had spent the day with a small boy at his private school, mounted their Rolls-Royce and drove away.

13

The artistic young men of Rackenbridge found themselves a good deal inconvenienced by Mrs Lace's preoccupation in her new love-affair. Their hearts were perhaps less affected than their stomachs, the emotions of those young men had never been much shaken by any petticoat, but up to now they had always been able to count on Comberry Manor and its chateleine for such agreeable amenities as free meals and pocket-money during the summer. This year a gloomy change had come about. The colony had already been at Rackenbridge for over a month, but as yet not one single picture, photograph, piece of pottery or hand-woven linen had been commissioned by their patroness, nor had she introduced to the studios, as she usually did, any gullible visitors. Almost worse than this trade depression was the fact that practically no invitations to meals at Comberry were now being issued. The artistic young men were getting tired of scrambled eggs and sardines eaten off studio floors, they longed to sit up to a table and attack a joint.

This state of affairs was rightly laid at Noel's door. As well as providing a complete distraction from the ordinary routine of her life he had shaken Mrs Lace in the belief that her friends were geniuses. He assured her that in London they were perfectly unknown, and his attitude towards their work, too, was distressing. For instance, after glancing at Mr Forderen's series of photographs entitled 'Anne-Marie in some of her exquisite moods' which, when they were first taken a year before had caused the greatest enthusiasm in Rackenbridge, he had remarked quite carelessly that she ought to have her photograph taken by some proper photographer.

'Don't you see,' Anne-Marie had said, 'that these pictures represent, not me but my moods, this one, for instance, "pensive by firelight", don't you think it rather striking?'

'No I don't,' said Noel, whose own mood that day was not of the sunniest. 'It is nothing but an amateurish snapshot of you looking affected. Frankly, I see no merit in any of them whatever, and as I said before, all those young aesthetes at Rackenbridge strike me as being fearfully 1923, and bogus at that.'

As a result of this conversation the series was removed from the walls of Anne-Marie's drawing-room, from whence it had long revolted Major Lace, and consigned to those of a downstairs lavatory. Here it was duly observed by poor Mr Forderen on the occasion of the cocktail-party.

Under the stress of these circumstances Rackenbridge abandoned the petty jealousies which usually marred its peace, and decided with unanimity upon a course of action. Mr Leader, who, up till now had been the envied but acknowledged favourite at Comberry Manor, was deputized to woo Mrs Lace away from her Philistine lover or, if this should not prove feasible, to point out at any rate that her old friends were entitled to some small part of her time and attention. To this end Mr Leader sent a little note accompanied by an offering of honey in a handmade jar, in which he begged Mrs Lace to keep a midnight assignation with him at a spot well known to them both, a little green knoll surmounted by a giant oak tree. He knew his Anne-Marie well enough to be convinced that whereas she might easily refuse to see him alone if he called in the ordinary way at six o'clock, the prospect of tearful scenes by moonlight would be beyond her powers to resist. Sure enough, at the very stroke of twelve o'clock she crept from her conjugal bed, leaving Major Lace to the company of his own tremendous snores which, as she well knew, nothing short of an earthquake could disturb. Throwing a chiffon wrap over her chiffon nightdress she floated away to join Mr Leader at his oak tree.

As she approached he took a graceful step forward, throwing out both his hands and cried, 'Beautiful Swan!' hoping thus to evoke romantic memories of a time when he and she were known in Rackenbridge as 'Leader and the Swan'. 'You look more lovely than I have ever seen you to-night. Are you a denizen of this earth, you wonderful creature, or do you come to us from another sphere!'

Anne-Marie, arranging herself upon the greensward, assumed a classical pose and gazed up at him with sombre eyes.

'I have com,' she said, her foreign accent more than usually stressed. 'It was dangerrous and de*ef feecult, but I have com. What ees it that you want – *que veux-tu mon ami?*'

'Everything,' said Mr Leader, moodily, 'or nothing.'

Anne-Marie leant back and waited for the passionate outburst which she hoped was coming; she was not disappointed. Mr Leader, assuming the attitude which had proved so successful when he as Hamlet and she as Ophelia had taken Rackenbridge by storm two years previously, began to accuse her of unfaithfulness, not to individuals, but to the deathless cause of Art. He told her that she alone could provide inspiration to those who loved her so earnestly, that no good work had been done at Rackenbridge that year, or could ever be done again until she should consent to shine like a star in their midst once more. As individuals they could bear her loss even if it killed them, as artists it was their duty to recall her to hers. Mr Leader spoke in this strain for some time, during which Anne-Marie wept and enjoyed it all very much, and particularly wished that Noel could have heard. When at last she had an opportunity to speak she said that those to whom she meant so much must make a tremendous effort to understand her now. She explained that she was probably one of the world's great lovers, and her love for Noel would be accounted in days to come as one of history's greatest loves.

'You must remember,' she said, gazing at the moon which hung over them like a large melon, 'that love, if it is to be worth while, is always tragic, always demands immense sacrifice. Otherwise it is of no value. I will sacrifice everything to it ruthlessly, my husband, my children, my reputation, éven all of you my friends, you and your wonderful work must go to feed the flames which light its altar. *Je n'en peux rien, que voulez-vous. C'est plus fort que la mort.*'

'How wonderful,' said Mr Leader, gloomily contrasting in his mind scrambled eggs and sardines with the very satisfying quality of Mrs Lace's food; 'but, dear Anne-Marie, can he be worthy of your exquisite intellect? We all greatly fear that he is not.'

'That may be so,' she said, complacently, 'but that is neither here nor there. What is intellect, compared with passion? I tell you that I love him, he occupies my time, my thoughts, my very soul – there is no room in my life for anybody else at the moment. When he is gone, as go he must, I may come back to all of you, an empty hollow husk; life will hold no more for me, but I shall at least have loved and made the great sacrifice, and I shall struggle on to the end, living for my memories.'

Her voice trailed away into a sob. Mr Leader, in the face of so much fortitude, and so much grief, found no words with which to suggest that a few free meals and one or two of the usual small commissions would be a great boon to himself, and his companions. He assured Anne-Marie that when her hour of sorrow should come she would find loving friends at Rackenbridge ready and anxious to pour balm into her wounds. Before he could enlarge upon this theme, Anne-Marie, whose trailing chiffon afforded but little warmth, and who was blue with cold, was floating back to that excellent circulation which, in her eyes, constituted Major Lace's chief virtue as a husband. Mr Leader sadly set forth on the long tramp to Rackenbridge.

One o'clock in the morning. The village of Chalford was sleeping soundly when a flickering light appeared in the sky and presently became a steady crimson glow. A reflection of it shone into Jasper's room, so he got up, very sleepy, and went out on to the green, looking to see where it could come from. In doing so he ran into Mr Leader, who was walking quickly towards Rackenbridge.

'Oh, hullo!' said Jasper, 'what is it, a house or a haystack?'

Mr Leader merely gave him a nasty look and hurried away.

Jasper, turning a corner of the village street, saw that Eugenia's Social Unionist head-quarters were a mass of flames. He felt sorry for Eugenia, he knew that she would be very much upset by this disaster. As it was a pretty sight, and he now felt fairly wide awake, he stayed to watch it blaze. Presently the others appeared, having been woken up by the smell of burning.

'Jolly little bonfire, isn't it?' said Jasper, putting his arm round Poppy's waist. 'Nothing we can do would be of any use, luckily. Hullo! here are the Comrades, rotten luck for them I must say.'

The Comrades marched up in formation, but seeing that no human effort would avail to extinguish that furnace, they indulged in a little community singing to keep up their spirits in the face of this setback to their cause.

Lady Marjorie, by the light of the flames, observed Mr Wilkins and with a little cry of excitement she streaked off in his direction.

'Wonderful, what love will do for a girl,' observed Jasper. 'I can't think when she finds time to grease her face nowadays; I suppose it will seize up soon, like a motor car. Hullo! here come the Laces to see the fun – goodbye, Noel. What did I say? This village is a perfect hot-bed of romance, isn't it, darling Miss Smith?' He kissed her ear. 'Oh, God! there are the detectives again; come on, let's bunk shall we? I'm sick of the sight of them.'

'Yes, in a way,' said Poppy. 'The only thing is, if they are still here it must mean that they haven't got any evidence on us.'

'I can't imagine why you don't hand out the dope and let the old boy divorce you if he wants to. It would save a lot of trouble.'

'Feminine caution, I suppose,' said Poppy. She was a good deal in love with Jasper, but not sure that she wanted to marry him. Certain aspects of his nature seemed far from satisfactory.

'He is such a fearful pickpocket, you know,' she said, in a burst of confidence to Marjorie. 'I can't leave my bag lying about for a moment.'

'Goodness knows how much he's had out of mine,' said Marjorie.

'Funny how customs have changed,' said Poppy. 'I'm sure in our mothers' day ladies didn't fall in love with thieves.'

Early next morning, Eugenia, on Vivian Jackson, came thundering down to the village at a hard gallop. Having inspected the still smouldering ruins of her head-quarters, she went round to the Jolly Roger, where she found Jasper and Noel eating breakfast in their pyjamas.

'It is a nuisance,' was all she said, but Jasper thought she had been crying. He plied her with sausages and she became more cheerful.

'Of course, it must be the work of Pacifists,' she said, with her mouth full, 'and you may be quite sure that I am going to sift this affair thoroughly. Wait until I have run them to earth, the brutal yellows financed by Jews too, no doubt.'

'Talking of Pacifists,' said Jasper, suddenly, 'whom do you think I saw last night hurrying away from your head-quarters just after the fire must have started? Dear little Mr Leader. He was behaving in a highly suspicious manner, I thought.'

Eugenia made that gesture which usually accompanies a snapping of the fingers. It was one she was very fond of, but as her hands were soft and babyish she seldom achieved a satisfactory crack. On this occasion it was completely absent.

'Mr Leader,' she cried, 'how mad of me, I had forgotten all about him. Of course, when we have a nest of filthy yellows in our midst, we need look no further afield. Very well, I shall act immediately.'

'What are you going to do?'

'I will send the Comrades to fetch him along,' said Eugenia. 'Terrible shall be the fate of the enemies of Social Unionism. In fact, I think I will arrange for the Comrades to seize him this very afternoon, while he is working in his STUDIO.' (She pronounced the word with infinite contempt.) 'He is probably laughing up his sleeve by now, thinking that nobody will ever find out who is the author of that foul crime. They can bind and gag him, and bring him to a quiet place I know of in Chalford Park, where I will court-martial him at the drumhead.'

'And if he is found guilty?'

'If,' cried Eugenia, tossing her head, 'there is no "if". He *shall* be found guilty and Oh, boy! will I have him beaten up? Terrible shall be the fate —'

Jasper, however, with some difficulty restrained her from putting such extreme proposals into practice. He explained that the time was not yet ripe for a blood-bath in Chalford, that such a proceeding would do infinite harm to her cause and that if she carried it out she would get herself into serious trouble with the Comrades at the London head-quarters. Those men of iron, he hinted, might easily degrade her from her position of patrol leader and remove her little emblem if she drew down upon them the unwelcome publicity that would follow such a step. It was this last argument which persuaded Eugenia to leave the whole matter in Jasper's hands.

'If he really did it, I think perhaps some small punishment is coming to him,' said Jasper, 'but it is absolutely essential that we should hear what he has to say for himself.'

'That's why we must have a trial,' said Eugenia, 'and you can't have a trial unless he is gagged and bound first. He is far too cunning and cowardly to put his head into the lion's den of his own accord.'

'We must consider it carefully,' said Jasper, 'there are probably ways and means.'

In the end, Lady Marjorie, whose passion for Mr Wilkins had brought her down from her high horse, and revealed her as a most surprisingly good-natured creature, allowed herself to be used as a decoy. She sent a note to Mrs Lace asking her to tea at the Jolly Roger. 'We hope *so* much that you will be able to come, Yours sincerely, Marjorie Merrith. PS. We wanted to invite also that charming Mr Leader whom we met at your cocktail-party, but cannot find out where he lives. Could you very kindly give him the message for us?'

'Very good indeed,' said Jasper, when this composition was submitted to him, 'I particularly like the use of the royal "We".'

Anne-Marie was pleased with her invitation. It was the first occasion on which she had been asked, except by Noel, to anything which was unconnected with the pageant, and privately she thought it was high time. Also she was pleased that Mr Leader had been included, and not her dreary husband. She had wished for some time that the Jolly Roger should make overtures to Rackenbridge. It would be so nice, she thought, if their inhabitants were to be merged into one Society for the Admiration of Mrs Lace. Besides, truth to tell, Noel's demeanour during the last few days had been slightly disquieting – he had seemed preoccupied and lacking in ardour. It would be an excellent stimulant for him to catch a glimpse of Mr Leader's breaking heart.

In fact, Noel was worrying. It was not his nature to live as Jasper did, from one day to another, picking up by fair means or foul enough cash for the needs of the moment and being dragged out of the bankruptcy courts about once every three years by protesting relations. He had always admired Jasper for this mode of life, envying the ease with which he could get something for nothing, and his eternal serenity, but was quite unable, at the last resort, to imitate him. His mother was a Scotchwoman and he, although hardly burdened with moral scruples, had inherited from her a care for the future. How often now did he curse himself for letting Jasper know of his legacy. This mad idea of pursuing unknown heiresses (he forgot that it had originated, in a moment of exaltation, from himself), would never have come to anything but for Jasper. When the first glow of excitement had died down he would have taken a cheap little holiday, perhaps in Spain, and then have returned to his job, happy in the extra security afforded him by the possession of a small capital. In time he would doubtless have achieved a partnership in his firm.

Under these circumstances it was specially irritating to observe that Jasper pursued, with great cheerfulness, his usual policy of living in the present. To see that jolly face one might suppose that there was no such thing as a day after tomorrow.

Noel, for his part, enjoyed nothing, not even his affair with Anne-Marie; he was tormented by the thought that his aunt's legacy was being frittered away with nothing to show for it, never considering that a happy time might be set off against the more material advantages which money can secure. He sent for his pass-book, and was overwhelmed with misery and self-reproach when he found that in one way and another four hundred pounds of his money had disappeared.

Nobody could fail to notice the gloom which enveloped him after this discovery and all put different constructions upon it. Jasper thought he had probably been gambling on the Stock Exchange; Poppy, that Mrs Lace was being tough to him; and Eugenia, that he had written an article for *The Union Jack* which had been turned down. This continually happened to her.

Mrs Lace begged in vain for his confidence. It was obvious in her mind that he must have received ill news from his own country, perhaps the regiments were proving unexpectedly loyal to the usurper, or could it be that Communism presented a greater menace than had at first been feared. She spent much of her time poring over her little girl's map of Europe and hazarding many a guess, but always ended up in a state of mystification. She was sadly deficient in general knowledge and was wont to declare that politics, and especially foreign politics were dreadfully boring compared to art and literature. Her reading of the newspapers was confined to the gossip columns, news about film stars, and such easily assimilated items of information as the birth in Dumfries-shire of a two-headed blackbird.

Noel was most unhelpful. If she threw out some hint such as 'I often think that it would be both interesting and enjoyable to visit the Balkans,' he would merely say, 'What an extraordinary idea, darling. It's a frightfully expensive journey, and nothing to do when you get there. I should have thought the South of France was more your dish.' At first, Mrs Lace felt herself to have been insulted by this remark; did he then suppose her to be a mere foolish butterfly searching for pleasure? Later on, however, having pondered over his words, she read another meaning into them. Perhaps, although unable to take his beloved with him to his own kingdom, he had it in mind to install her in some gorgeous villa on the Riviera, where he could visit her when on holiday. She felt that an arrangement of this description would suit her very well, as she was partial both to dagoes and sunbathing. She wondered whether it would be too much to ask for a flat in Paris as well.

Mrs Lace had some difficulty in luring Mr Leader to the Jolly Roger. He felt instinctively that these new people who had come to upset the whole summer would be unlikely to accept him at his own valuation and he very much objected to the company of anybody who might prove to be his intellectual superior. In the end, Mrs Lace managed to persuade him that he had better come with her by hinting that he might be commissioned to design dresses for the pageant, which surely would not go against his conscience so long as he was well paid. He saw the force of this argument, and besides, it was not really in his nature to resist free food.

When they arrived at the Jolly Roger they found the party already sitting round a tea-table in the garden. It consisted of Marjorie, Poppy, Eugenia, Jasper and Mr Wilkins. Noel was not there, having been obliged to go to London for the day. Mrs Lace was annoyed by his absence but concealing the fact she sat down beside Jasper. There was no chair for poor Mr Leader, who was obliged to fetch one for himself out of the parlour. Poppy and Lady Marjorie then made him sit between them, and asked him, with every demonstration of friendliness, why he and his friends had not undertaken an episode in the pageant.

'Our political principles forbid,' said Mr Leader. 'Thank you, I like it very weak, with no milk or sugar, also we are busy men.'

'So busy,' said Eugenia, coming straight to the charge, 'that you still haven't been to see the inside of our Social Unionist head-quarters.'

'Not yet,' said Mr Leader.

'Did you know that they have been burnt down?' she inquired, staring at him with eyes like enormous blue headlamps.

'Have they really? I say, bad luck.'

'Thank you, we don't want your sympathy, we want to know what you were doing the night before last?'

Mrs Lace looked anxiously at Mr Leader.

'Really, I have no idea at all. What were you doing yourself?'

'Don't be impertinent,' said Eugenia, stiffly. 'It is curious, is it not, that you, a well-known Pacifist, should have been observed retreating guiltily from the scene of incendiarism shortly after the fire began. How do you explain this coincidence?'

Mr Leader silently waited for Anne-Marie to provide his alibi. Anne-Marie did no such thing. She was far from anxious that Noel on the one hand, or Major Lace on the other, should know of her midnight rendezvous. If it were to be disclosed at this table, Noel would certainly hear it from Jasper, and Major Lace from Mr Wilkins. She could not take the risk.

'Answer,' said Eugenia, sternly, 'and answer truthfully. Lies shall not avail you here.'

Mrs Lace now turned to Jasper, and said, 'How absurd. That child's passion for play-acting is great fun of course, but doesn't it make her behave in rather a babyish way sometimes?'

'If Eugenia suspects a chap of burning down her head-quarters,' said Jasper, 'I think it is only fair to them both that he should be questioned and given a chance to clear himself. After all, he was behaving rather suspiciously that night. What have you to say, Leader?'

Mr Leader held his peace.

'As I thought,' remarked Eugenia, 'Van der Lubbe, I always felt that here was no Dimitroff.'

At this insult Mr Leader got up and left the party.

Mrs Lace, if she felt inclined to follow her friend, who after all had stood by her with some courage, made no move to do so. She must, whatever the cost, keep on good terms with Eugenia until the Grand Social Unionist rally, pageant and garden party was over. Not for any loyalty was she going to sacrifice her chance of riding in that coach.

She now chattered gaily about many things, supplementing her remarks with a wealth of gestures, and presently asked Jasper why that naughty Noel had gone to London so suddenly.

'That is a state secret,' said Jasper.

She looked at him significantly, and then, lowering her voice, she said, 'How goes it?'

'Only too well,' said Jasper.

'He tells me nothing.'

'He is afraid – of spoiling things for you.'

'This silence is hard to bear.'

'A woman's lot is often hard. You must have courage.'

'When will he have to leave?'

'¿Quien sabe?'

Mrs Lace wondered whether Lady Marjorie and Mrs St Julien were in the secret, not that it would help her much if they were. She would never be able to worm anything out of them, even if pride permitted her to make the attempt.

'I wonder,' she said to Jasper, still in an undertone, 'if you would write down his motto for me. I thought of having some little memento made for him, a little keepsake, and I should like to have his motto engraved on it.'

'Certainly,' said Jasper, who had been finding out one or two things from Mr Wilkins of late. He took the paper and pencil that she offered and wrote. 'Bella, Horrida Bella.' Over these words he drew a crown of exaggerated dimensions. Mrs Lace folded the paper carefully and placed it in her bag. She thought it a wonderfully romantic coincidence that her own name should be incorporated in the royal motto of Noel's ancestors.

'By the way,' said Poppy, breaking in on these confidences, 'I have been meaning for ages to ask you whether you have made out that list of neighbours for Cousin Maud Chalford? I think she is depending on it, and the invitations must be sent during the next day or two, because the time really is getting rather short.'

Lady Marjorie asked Mr Wilkins if he wasn't living for the pageant and Mr Wilkins said that he supposed he was.

'I can't wait,' said Lady Marjorie.

'But I'm afraid you'll have to,' said Mr Wilkins, who liked to stress the obvious.

'The list is quite ready,' said Mrs Lace. 'I brought it with me so that Eugenia can give it to Lady Chalford without any more delay.'

'Do let me see,' said Lady Marjorie. 'Oh, good! Wilma Alexander. Of course, I forgot that she lives near here – the Faircombes too. I say, Poppy, there are masses of people we know on this list, will it matter, d'you think?'

'I don't suppose they'll recognize us in our fancy dresses.'

'Well, it can't be helped if they do. I really can't live the whole rest of my life in disguise on account of Osborne.' She went on perusing the list.

'The episodes are all arranged for, now,' Jasper told Mrs Lace. 'Each branch of Social Unionism in the county is responsible for one. There will be nearly three hundred Comrades acting, as far as I can make out, for whom we have to provide clothes. We shall have to call a committee meeting to discuss it.

'Then Miss Trant, the organist, has had a wonderful idea. She thinks we should have an Olde Englyshe Fayre going on at the same time, and she is arranging Maypole dances and art needlework stalls and so on.'

'Oh! surely,' said Mrs Lace, 'Olde Englyshe things are rather a bore, aren't they? I should have thought that we want to keep an eighteenth-century spirit? Why not a Regency Rout for example?'

'We like Olde Englyshe best,' said Jasper, 'because it is so wonderfully funny. Besides, a pageant must be kept thoroughly lowbrow or it loses all character.'

'Miss Trant is being very kind and helpful. She is so sweet,' said Poppy. 'Do you know her?'

Mrs Lace had spent the eight years of her married life patronizing Miss Trant, whom she regarded as a stupid, common little woman, second only in dreariness to Mr Wilkins. There seemed no end to the pin-pricks which poor Mrs Lace was doomed to endure.

Eugenia, who had sat in silence, munching a twopenny bar, since the departure of Mr Leader, now said she must be off. She hailed Vivian Jackson, who appeared from nowhere, took Mrs Lace's list of the neighbours, kicked up the Reichshund, who was snoring in the sun; and, still munching, she trotted away. That evening Mr Leader was dragged from his bed by masked men wearing Union Jack shirts and flung into an adjacent duck pond. As the weather was extremely hot he took no chill and suffered nothing worse than a little mortification and the loss of his *eau-de-nil* pyjama trousers. Nobody else witnessed the affair and Mr Leader did not take any legal or other steps. Nevertheless, the seed was sown of an active resentment against Social Unionism and his treacherous enchantress, Mrs Lace.

14

Lady Chalford sent her motor car to the Jolly Roger with a message that she wished to see Mrs St Julien and Mr Aspect on a matter of extreme importance, and would be greatly obliged if they would come to Chalford House immediately. The car would wait to take them. They entered it with some trepidation, feeling very much like naughty children and wondering which particular enormity had been found out.

When they arrived however, their minds were set at rest on this score; T.P.O.F. was in an almost hysterical mood, but not on account of anything they had done.

'Dear child, dear Mr Aspect,' she said, waving the list of neighbours at them, 'I need your advice, a really dreadful thing has happened – I don't know when I have felt so much upset. On reading this list I am horrified and disgusted to see that there is nobody on it (not a single soul) whom I could possibly ask inside my house. Do you know that when I had been through it twice I could scarcely believe that there was not some mistake, so I sent for my husband's agent and he assured me that it is perfectly accurate, every family for miles round is mentioned on it. I had no idea that we lived in such a shocking neighbourhood.'

'Really,' said Poppy, with interest, 'why, whatever is the matter with them all?'

'The matter?' said Lady Chalford, in a voice of bewilderment, 'the matter is that none of them are respectable. I really cannot understand it. Since I stopped going out of course some of the houses have changed hands, but for all that a great many are still occupied by the same families as the ones I used to know quite well, and who were ordinary decent people like you or me. Since those days the most shocking, distressing things seem to have taken place.'

'What sort of things?'

'My dear, you may well ask. I tell you this list has upset me more than I can say. Take any name from it at random – they are all alike, they all have some sort of cloud hanging over them. Take for instance the first name, the Alexanders. The late Lord Alexander, my dear husband's closest friend for many years, has been succeeded at Bruton Park by his eldest son, Lord Bruton whom, as a child, I often held in my arms. Now, what do I learn? This unfortunate young man has been trapped into marriage with a woman years older than himself, a woman from the variety stage; what is called, I believe, a *cabaret* artiste.'

Poppy gave half a look in Jasper's direction and they both checked a giggle. Trapped into marriage was hardly the expression to use of Lord Alexander, who was well known to have pursued his lovely wife over three continents before she would make up her mind to marry him.

'But you know,' said Poppy, 'Wilma Alexander is awfully respectable and the sweetest person in the world. You'd love her. They are as happy as kings and she is quite wrapped up in Bertie and the children.'

'My dear, I am prepared to believe anything you tell me about this Lady Alexander, but I have no intention of inviting her to my house. She may, for all I know, be a most excellent wife and mother, such women sometimes are. But the fact remains that she could never be a suitable friend for a young girl like Eugenia. I don't want you to think that I am being unduly particular however, so I am now going to read out a few more examples from this unsavoury document.' Lady Chalford adjusted her spectacles and continued, 'Here we have the Hon. Adrian and Mrs Duke; Mrs Duke, it appears, is the divorced wife of a colonel, so these two people are in fact living together adulterously.'

'Dodo wasn't divorced,' said Poppy, 'she divorced her husband, who was a perfect brute to her.'

'I am surprised that you should think it makes any difference. "Till death us do part", is the vow. If her husband was cruel to her she could apply for a separation and live in decent retirement for the rest of her life. Pray, my dear, do not interrupt me. Here we have Mr John Shipton, grandson of a man who was publicly accused, in his clubs, of cheating at billiards. I well remember the incident, which caused a great deal of unpleasantness at the time; he was, of course, obliged to leave the country. Now, although it is not the fault of this Mr Shipton that he was born into such a family, and although he may be most respectable himself, I cannot risk inviting him here. Bad blood usually comes out sooner or later, and it is impossible to be over careful where a young girl like dearest Eugenia is concerned. Sir Archibold and Lady Faircombe, poor things, have a divorced daughter who runs a dress-shop in London – not very nice, is it? Major Montgomerie's son was expelled from Eton – in my day when such a disgrace fell upon a family it was usual for them to go and settle in some colony. Mr Newman's mother was half German and my husband very rightly refuses to have anyone of German extraction inside the house. Lord George Fairbrother is a well-known drunkard and people say that General Parsley had to leave his regiment on account of gambling debts. I won't bore you with any further accounts of such dreadful people, there are dozens of them on this paper and I can assure you that it is one long sordid tale of vice, drunkenness and gaming too terrible to think about. I'm sure I don't know what it is that has come over this unfortunate neighbourhood; anybody might suppose it had been cursed.'

It was now quite evident to Poppy and Jasper that Lady Chalford could not be right in the head; her long seclusion, they supposed, had affected her sanity. She must be humoured.

Poppy said, gently, 'What a dreadful state of affairs, Cousin Maud. Now, you must tell us what you would like us to do about the pageant and garden party on the sixteenth.'

'That is exactly what I have been so worried about,' said Lady Chalford, pathetically. 'After all the trouble you have taken I don't wish you to be disappointed, and Eugenia, poor child, has set her heart on this pageant. I think her Scouts or Guides or Comrades or whatever she calls them have all been working very hard too, and I am particularly glad to see that she is doing something for the village at last. I never used to be able to make her feel the smallest interest until she joined this Movement, whatever it is. So, taking all that into consideration, I have decided that, although it would be out of the question now to entertain my neighbours at a garden party, there is no reason why the pageant should not take place. We will throw open the park on that day, charging a small sum for charity, and like this your time will not have been wasted, and my little Eugenia will not be disappointed.'

'That is much the best plan,' said Poppy, soothingly.

'But, alas! now I am as far as ever from solving the future of my poor little grandchild.'

'She is very young,' said Jasper, 'and I expect you will find that her future will arrange itself quite satisfactorily.'

Lady Chalford gave him a searching look. She seemed about to say something, but refrained.

As he walked home with Poppy through Chalford Park, Jasper said: 'The poor old female is evidently as stupid as an owl and as blind as a bat. She thinks I'm going to marry Eugenia and what's more she likes the idea. Somehow I shouldn't have imagined, from what I know of her moral standards, that I was at all her dish, quite the contrary.'

'Perhaps her estate agent doesn't know much about you yet.'

'Maybe. I'm bound to say I think she has some exceedingly odd views on the subject of social relationships. She ostracizes all the chaps that have had tough luck, like being caught out cheating at billiards or having lousy husbands, whereas one knows she wouldn't mind a scrap if they did really wicked things like grinding down the poor. I believe that our generation has far better ethical values than hers had; we see the chaps we like, even if they are hell, and avoid the ones we don't. It's the only sensible criterion, don't you agree, Miss Smith?'

'You can't talk about ethical values and moral standards,' said

Poppy, bitterly, 'because you don't know the meaning of such things.'

'I'm a nicer guy than you seem to think,' said Jasper, carelessly. 'I never do anybody much harm, and I'm loyal to my friends when it comes to the point.'

'I don't notice you being specially loyal to the wretched Noel.'

'That's where you're wrong. Nobody understands about me and Noel; ours is a very complicated relationship which began nearly twenty years ago when we were new boys together at our private. It is chiefly based on the fact that Noel expects a certain type of treatment from me, he would be very much put out if he got any other. The truth is that he gets a great deal of vicarious pleasure out of my evil doings. For instance, he likes having me down here, enjoys my company and so on; but what he positively adores is the feeling that he is forced to keep me here by the most unprincipled blackmail on my part. It wouldn't be a quarter the satisfaction to him if I were to pay for myself like any ordinary person, because then I shouldn't be living up to his conception of my character.'

'I suppose that's one way of looking at it,' said Poppy, doubtfully.

'Besides, think what a wonderfully good turn I did him with that old Local Beauty. Why, the girl was gunning for me, you know, as hard as she could, but after half an hour's conversation with me she turned right about and started gunning for Noel instead, and from that day to this she has never looked back once. No, you can't pretend that I'm disloyal.'

'I shouldn't call it a sign of loyalty to throw anyone into the arms of that awful, affected, pretentious Mrs Lace.'

'Bella, Horrida Bella? I think she's quite a cup of tea. But the point is, you don't know the old boy like I do. The only love that counts for a row of pins from his point of view is the hopeless sort. As soon as a girl begins to be able to sit in the same room with him he sheers off. If the old L.B., or Local Beauty, had still been after me, he would still have been mad about her, as it is, he is cooling down wonderfully. Darling Miss Smith, now you might as well admit that I am a loyal guy.'

'All right, my poppet, don't make such a to-do. I expect even you have got a few good qualities, everybody has. I was only suggesting that, judged by the usual standards, you are a bit of a burglar.'

'Oh! well,' said Jasper gloomily, 'if that's all – a chap has got to live somehow you know, it's one long struggle to survive in one's environment. But look here, why don't you marry me? I'll promise to give up being a burglar and work for my living some other way – how about that?'

'We'll see,' said Poppy. 'I don't really approve of marriage, you know. I think settlements are the thing to go for, these days.'

'Why did you marry Anthony St Julien?'

'How stupid you are. A girl must marry once, you can't go on being called Miss – Miss all your life, it sounds too idiotic. All the same, marriage is a great bore – chap's waistcoats lying about in one's bedroom, and so on. It gets one down in time. Hullo! Look! here come Eugenia and Vivian Jackson. Hail!' she cried.

'Hail, Union Jackshirts!' Eugenia trotted up to them and dismounted, sending Vivian Jackson about his business with a tremendous whack on the hind-quarters, 'have you been to see T.P.O.F.? She was in an awful stew when I left.'

'We have,' said Poppy, 'and she's calmed down again nicely.'

'Yes,' said Eugenia anxiously, 'but what did you arrange?'

'It's all right. There's to be no tee-d up garden party, but the pageant is to take place just the same, with a small charge for admission.'

'Oh! good,' said Eugenia, greatly relieved. 'That makes it all the easier for us to have our Grand S.U. rally. I must begin to see about the posters and leaflets – I thought we might distribute some Social Unionist hymns and propaganda while we are about it.'

'T.P.O.F. seems quite enthusiastic about Union Jackshirtism.'

'Yes, she thinks it's the Women's Institute and she's all for it. Keeps on saying how pleased she is that I do something for the village at last. Nanny's the one who hates it so much. I'm always afraid she's going to tell on me, the old Pacifist.'

'I shouldn't think she'd do that.'

'She'd better not, unless she wants to be beaten up by the Comrades.'

There was a pause in the conversation. Eugenia began to hum, as she often did, the tune of *'Deutschland Deutschland Uber Alles!'* to which she sang the substituted words, 'Union Jackshirts Up and At 'Em, Push their faces in the mud!'

Presently Jasper said: 'Poppy and I were just talking about getting married.'

'To whom?'

'To each other, dear.'

Eugenia looked at them severely. 'If cousin Poppy St Julien had the true principles of Social Unionism at heart she would return to her husband and present him with several healthy male children.'

'Darling Eugenia,' cried Poppy, 'he wouldn't like that a bit. Why, when I think of all the trouble I've taken —'

'Is your husband an Aryan?'

'I really don't quite know what an Aryan is.'

'Well, it's quite easy. A non-Aryan is the missing link between man and beast. That can be proved by the fact that no animals, except the Baltic goose, have blue eyes.'

'How about Siamese cats?' said Jasper.

'That's true. But Siamese cats possess, to a notable degree, the Nordic virtue of faithfulness.'

'Indeed they don't,' said Poppy. 'We had one last summer and he brought back a different wife every night. Even Anthony was quite shocked.'

Eugenia was in no way put out. 'I know, they may not be faithful to non-Aryan cats,' she said, 'why should they be? But they love their Nordic owners, and even go for long walks with them.'

'So your definition of an Aryan is somebody who will go for long walks with other Aryans? Come on now, Miss Smith, does Anthony St Julien go for long walks with you or is he the missing link?'

'Union Jackshirt Aspect,' said Eugenia sharply, 'no levity, please.' She turned to Poppy and said, 'If your husband is an Aryan you should be able to persuade him that it is right to live together and breed; if he is a filthy non-Aryan it may be your duty to leave him and marry Jackshirt Aspect. I am not sure about this, we want no immorality in the Movement . . .'

'It's quite all right,' said Jasper, 'you can take it from me that Anthony St Julien is a very low type, there is nothing of the Baltic goose about him.'

Eugenia paid no attention. 'I have just been to see Union Jackshirt Foster and was obliged to speak to him about his association with Mrs Lace. It may, of course, be perfectly innocent, but it causes much talk in the village, so my Comrades tell me. It must come to an end therefore; at best it gives the Pacifists a peg on which they may hang libellous statements about the party to which Union Jackshirt Foster belongs, at worst he may be luring her away from her duty as the wife and mother of Aryans.'

'Well, well, what a governessy little thing it is,' said Jasper. 'So what had Union Jackshirt Foster to say for himself?'

'His statement was neither satisfactory nor convincing,' replied Eugenia, 'in fact, I shall be obliged to write a request for his formal resignation from the Movement to-night.'

'I don't know which is the worse, you or T.P.O.F.'

'This country must be purged of petty vice before it can be fit to rule the world,' cried Eugenia. She remounted Vivian Jackson and galloped away.

'That's a fine girl,' said Jasper. 'If she had been born twenty years sooner she would have been a suffragette.'

15

Jasper and Noel sat in the bar, deserted by their women kind who were at Comberry Manor trying on dresses for the pageant. They drank quantities of beer and talked about themselves, the conversation having opened in a tone of extreme cordiality. It appeared that Noel was now rather uncomfortably involved in the affair Lace; Anne-Marie, having abandoned that philosophical serenity which he had found so unusual and so admirable, had recently embarked upon a series of painful scenes. Major Lace, too, according to his wife, was both jealous and suspicious, and trouble was to be anticipated from that quarter.

'Of course I was a fool to imagine it,' Noel said drearily, 'but she honestly did seem a bit different from other girls. I must try and remember another time that they are all the same in the end.'

'The great thing about women,' said Jasper, 'is that they have a passion for getting relationships cut and dried. It seems to be their first object in life. If they are having an ordinary love-affair they can't be happy until they have turned it into a romance of the till-death-us-do-part description, while matrimony, even in these days, is never as far as it might be from the back of their minds. They are wonderfully adept at herding chaps into that particular pen, no method is too dishonest which achieves that end. If they are themselves unmarried they pretend that their mother has forbidden them to see one, if married that the husband is getting jealous, until, maddened by all these restrictions, one ends by proposing. Of course neither mother nor husband would have the smallest idea that anything unusual was going on if the little darlings weren't continually dropping dark hints. Oh! what maddening creatures. I do envy people whose tastes lie in any other direction. All the same,' he added, 'I'm bound to say that my Miss Smith seems exceptional in that respect.'

'Don't you believe it,' said Noel, cheerfully, 'she's just leaving a side door open in case she can persuade that husband of hers to take her back.'

'Blast you,' said Jasper gloomily. He had long suspected as much himself.

'Anyway,' continued Noel, 'she has one great advantage – she does at least realize that you can't afford to marry. I wish to goodness I could convince Anne-Marie the same about me – that ring was a bad tactical error on my part, ever since I gave it to her she seems to suppose that I am vastly rich. Why, what on earth do you think she suggested this morning? That I should buy a villa for her in the south of France, if you please, and install her there as my mistress! The girl must be wrong in the head.'

Jasper giggled. 'I think that's funny.'

'It's not funny for me,' said Noel, 'I'm getting too much tied up altogether and it's damned tiresome I can tell you. As soon as this pageant is over I'm jolly well going to cut and run.'

'Where to?'

'Back to my old job at Fruel's again, I suppose,' said Noel drearily, 'as I seem to have ratted all these heiresses I shall be obliged to go on working for my living.' As he said these words a horrid vision rose before his eyes of Miss Brisket the plain typist, Miss Clumps the pretty one, and the ferret eyes and astute nose of Mr Farmer the head clerk. They were framed in olde oake and stained glass, and looked like demons in hell waiting to torment him.

Jasper's voice recalled him to earth. 'Actually,' it was saying, 'I don't think you'll be going back to Fruel's.'

'Oh? Why not?'

'Because when I was up in London the other day I went round to New Broad Street and had a chat with Sir Percy. I explained to him that I am really in many ways more suited to that particular line of business than you are, and do you know he quite saw my point – quite. Charming and intelligent man, Sir Percy. He told me that you had left for good this time. I begin work on the first of next month.'

Noel paled. The vision which had seemed so devilish a moment ago recurred to him with a strangely altered aspect. Miss Brisket, Miss Clumps and Mr Farmer, in their old-world setting, now appeared as angels of light, singing to welcome the pilgrims of the night.

'Jasper,' he said bitterly, 'I always knew you were the biggest swine I knew, but I never knew quite what a swine you were until now.'

'My dear old boy,' said Jasper, in pained surprise, raising his eyebrows very high, 'now don't let's have any ill feeling about this, please. You had definitely resigned, hadn't you? As jobs go it's a good job, and it seemed only sensible to keep it in the family, so to speak. Honestly, old boy, I'm most exceedingly sorry that you are upset about this, but I'm bound to say I don't see what you're complaining of.'

'All right,' said Noel suddenly, 'as you've got my job and as you're welcome to my share of Mrs Lace, you can't do me any more dirt, so I can stop paying your bills in this lousy hole. That's one comfort. Here, miss! Put all these beers down to room 8, will you?'

For once in his life Jasper was left with nothing to say.

After this Noel began taking steps to find himself work. He stayed on at Chalford because he was infected with the general excitement over the pageant, and besides London at the moment was hot and empty of influential people. So he wrote letters. He felt that it was useless to hope for an invitation to resume his old position in the office of Fruel and Grimthorpe; after the barbed shafts which had doubtless been inserted into the mind of Sir Percy Fruel by Jasper, an application there would only be made at the risk of a colossal snub. Noel therefore wrote to his three uncles, all of whom occupied good positions in the world of finance. He explained that he was wasting his time in a stock-broker's office, it was an occupation which he felt gave him too little scope for his talents. He would prefer some job where he could make use of his languages and his rather special knowledge of central European conditions. If Jasper can bluff his way through life, he thought, as he wrote this, so should I be able to. The uncles, he knew, rightly regarded him as a young man who, while lacking in brilliance, could be relied upon to execute anything he might be given to do with steady industry. They had for years deprecated his friendship with the notorious Mr Aspect and might be very much inclined to assist him to a job abroad, far from that malign influence. Noel also thought that once away from Chalford it would be no bad thing to put the German ocean between himself and Mrs Lace for a time. Whilst awaiting developments however, he continued to dally with that lady, to whose attractions he was perhaps not quite so insensible as he liked to imagine.

'How very mysterious,' said Poppy, who, accompanied by Jasper, had just returned from a rehearsal of the Chalford group's episode. It was the last but one before the pageant and had been a heavy failure. 'How very mysterious, here's an enormous parcel for me. It is strange, as nobody knows I'm here, except I suppose Anthony, and he wouldn't be likely to send me a parcel.'

'No, only a writ,' said Jasper.

'So queer,' Poppy continued. 'It's not my birthday or anything either, besides, nobody gets a post here ever, except the detectives.' She pulled at its brown paper wrapping, 'Why, it's just like a very heavy hat box, registered too. I simply don't understand it.'

When at last she had made a hole in the brown paper, which was of a particularly tough brand, a neat wooden box was revealed, clearly needing hammer and chisel to open it. Jasper, who was by now almost as curious as Poppy, went off and borrowed these implements from Mr Birk.

'It's exactly the sort of box my wedding presents used to arrive in,' said Poppy, hovering round while Jasper bashed away at it. 'Somebody always used to injure themselves opening them, and then one would plough one's way through oceans of shavings in order to reveal some awful little glass inkstand. How I used to cry when I was engaged.'

'I'm not surprised. Marriage with old missing link St Julien can't have been a very pretty future for a nice Nordic girl like you to contemplate.'

'Hullo!' said Poppy, 'so what did I tell you? Oceans of shavings. How like old times – now for the inkpot.'

Inside the shavings was a large red leather case.

'Whoever sent this wasn't going to risk having their precious inkpot broken.'

Inside the large red leather case was a large diamond tiara.

Poppy and Jasper blinked. They looked at each other and looked again at the tiara and neither spoke. After a few minutes Poppy placed it carefully on the hall table and removing her gaze from it with some reluctance she began to search once more among the shavings. This she did in the purely mechanical manner of one whose reflexes have been conditioned to a particular reaction on the receipt of diamond tiaras. She soon found what she was looking for, a visiting-card. The name engraved upon it was the name of Jasper's grandfather, and on it was written in pencil, 'To a very charming little lady from an old friend, who hopes that soon he may boast a more intimate relationship.'

Jasper took it from her and read it in his turn.

'Good,' he said comfortably, 'now we really shall be able to be married.'

Poppy, who was trying on the tiara in front of a looking-glass, said, 'Why?'

'On the proceeds, silly.'

'Proceeds of what? I don't somehow think I intend to sell my tiara,' said Poppy, 'if that's what you mean.' She twisted her head about to make it sparkle. 'Really, it suits me a treat, doesn't it?'

'Remember you are going to be a poor man's wife, you can't afford these expensive treats.'

'Yes, but if I stay with Anthony St Julien I can afford them easily.'

'Well, I'm bound to say that's pretty cool. If you stay with

Anthony St Julien it is to be hoped you will be sufficiently honourable to hand over that tiara.'

'To whom, pray?'

'To me, of course. After all, the old boy sent it along as a wedding present for me, didn't he?'

'I don't agree at all. Just read that card again and show me one single mention either of you or of a wedding on it. I might possibly return it to the duke, but it has nothing to do with you.'

'Here look,' said Jasper, holding up the card, '"who hopes he may soon boast a more intimate relationship with her." How about that?'

'I hope the duke has honourable intentions,' said Poppy carelessly. She picked up the tiara and put it back into its case, and then, still holding it, she walked through the hall, 'Mr Birk!' she called.

Mr Birk appeared from his parlour.

'Could I borrow your car now, at once? I want to go to the bank at Rackenbridge.'

'Yes, by all means, Miss Smith.'

'It's after five now,' said Jasper, 'banks shut at three, you know, dear.' Mr Birk looked from one to the other. Poppy said to him, 'I have got a piece of jewellery here that I am very anxious to see safely locked up, Mr Birk. Do you think there is any way I could get hold of the bank manager?'

'Yes, certainly, Miss Smith. As it happens the manager is my wife's brother – I will drive you into Rackenbridge myself, and see to it. I'm sure he will do anything to oblige you. If you will wait a moment I will go and start the car.'

'Thank you very much,' said Poppy, 'I will come round to the garage with you.' A few minutes later she could be seen driving off in the direction of Rackenbridge, still clutching the precious red leather case.

That Jane has learnt a thing or two since she has been down here, thought Jasper, with some admiration. He turned automatic steps towards the bar where he was met by Mrs Birk.

'Excuse me troubling you, sir,' she said, 'but here is your account for last week. Mr Foster told us that yours is to be kept separate as from last Thursday.'

'Oh! yes, thanks,' said Jasper. The bill seemed to him enormous. He read the items, recognized with a sigh that they were correct, and wrote out a cheque for the amount, which he handed airily to Mrs Birk.

'A double whisky, please,' he added.

16

The countryside for many miles round Chalford was now made hideous by enormous posters, carefully printed out by hand in black ink, which for weeks past had occupied the leisure hours of Eugenia and her Comrades, and which combined a little discreet propaganda with the announcement that a Grand Social Unionist Rally, Pageant, Garden Party and Olde Englyshe Fayre would take place at Chalford House. The gates would be open at 2.30 p.m. on the Wednesday following, entrance 1s. Eugenia pointed out to Jasper the true *chic* of these posters which lay in the fact that no two were alike.

'Oh really, aren't they?' said Jasper, 'but I thought they looked exactly the same – anyway, they all seem to have a picture of King Kong on them.'

'How stupid you are,' said Eugenia, angrily fingering her dagger, 'can't you see that's a Union Jackshirt Comrade handing on the torch of Social Unionism to the youth of Britain? They all have that, I mean that the wording of each is different, according to where it is to be hung. Haven't you read the one outside the Jolly Roger for instance?'

'I didn't read it,' said Jasper, 'because I was too busy admiring King – I mean the Union Jackshirt Comrade.'

'Well, you should. It refers to the decadence of high society in these post-War days, pointing out that its members are no longer of any value to the community as they possess neither moral sense nor political integrity. That's meant for all of you.'

'Oh, thanks, I'm sure,' said Jasper.

'The posters in Rackenbridge speak of the yellow hand of the Pacifist incendiaries, and how the fate of Van der Lubbe will surely o'ertake all enemies to the Social Unionist cause. There is one on

Major Lace's big cowshed comparing our agricultural policy with that of jelly-breasted Tory politicians, and explaining that agriculture will be nationalized under the régime and farmers allowed no longer to muddle about in their own way. The one on the vicarage wall says that whereas religion has failed so notably in this country Social Unionism will soon be here to take its place, the one on Mr Isaac's house promises that all Jews will be sent to live in Jerusalem the Golden with milk and honey blest, and the one on Lord Alexander's park gates has information with regard to the obsolete nature of hereditary legislation.'

'I expect you must be making yourself most wonderfully popular in these paris.'

'What is popularity?' cried Eugenia with contempt. 'What is life itself compared to The Flag? The Comrades are simply thrilled for Wednesday. I can't tell you,' she went on, 'how splendidly they have arranged everything. Seven big charabancs full of Union Jackshirts are expected, and they are all coming over for the dress-rehearsal on Monday as well. Those who aren't actually performing are going to dress-up in the proper clothes of the period and help swell the cheering for George the Third. Oh, bother! it is really too bad we have got to have Mrs Lace in that coach.'

'Never mind, you will have to concentrate on Mr Wilkins, he seems to be quite an enthusiastic member now.'

'Yes, that's one comfort. I'm going to ask him if he will wear his little emblem on his robes, after all George the Third was a sort of prophet, wasn't he?'

'Quite batty, I believe,' said Jasper.

'Miss Trant has been wonderful,' continued Eugenia, 'I can't think what we should have done without her to help us. She has managed to hire a hundred Dolly Varden and a hundred Dresden Shepherd costumes for only half a crown each, and she is organizing the tea. I must go now and write out post cards to remind all branches concerned that the dress-rehearsal will be at 2 p.m. on Monday, not 3 as originally settled. Oh! you do think it's going to be a success Union Jackshirt Aspect, don't you?'

'I am certain that it will prove a highly entertaining afternoon,' said Jasper. She trotted away on her little black horse. 'Yes, Mr Birk?' 'So sorry to trouble you,' said Mr Birk. He held in his hand a cheque, which Jasper had no difficulty in recognizing as the one with which he had paid Mrs Birk some days previously. 'This has been sent back R/D,' said Mr Birk, 'there must be some mistake.'

Jasper took it, glanced at it casually and said, 'Oh, I see, a small misunderstanding no doubt. How stupid of my bank, I suppose I shall have to go and send a telegram to that fool of a manager.'

He strolled away in the direction of the post office, where he sent a telegram to his sister, urging her to wire him ten pounds, signing it 'S.O.S. Jasper'. He felt low. Poppy still pursued her plan of keeping him on tenterhooks so that he had no idea whether she also was emotionally committed or not. The detectives had left Chalford, vanishing as suddenly and as mysteriously as they had appeared, and this seemed to be worrying her. 'It looks as though they have the evidence they wanted,' she said. 'We were mad not to be more careful.' Jasper thought that there could be nothing in the world so depressing as financial troubles coupled with emotional uncertainty. He very much hoped, incidentally, that his sister would not have gone abroad yet.

Noel now accentuated Jasper's sufferings by suddenly assuming the demeanour of excessive cheerfulness. He boasted continually of wonderful jobs which his uncles were going to find for him on the Continent. They had, in fact, written to him quite kindly on this subject, and he was expecting any day to hear more definitely from one or other of them.

Hopeful of this he kept Mrs Lace at bay with vague but interesting promises, an achievement which was not at the moment very difficult, as all her thoughts and energies were concentrated on the pageant. So engrossed was she with dreams of the great day near at hand that she never noticed the unusual behaviour of the Rackenbridge young men. Mr Leader cut her in the High Street one morning, Mr Forderen had not even answered a letter in which she had invited him to photograph her in some eighteenth-century moods. It did not occur to her to conclude from these and other omens that Rackenbridge might be making its own plans for Wednesday afternoon.

The day before the pageant broke in a downpour which was perfectly solid and had every appearance of being the sort that lasts for a week at least.

'Set in for wet,' said Mr Birk cheerfully, whistling between his teeth. The weather forecast in the *Daily Mail* supported him in this dreary prophecy; 'Further outlook uncertain,' it said.

Poppy, Marjorie, Jasper and Noel herded together in the parlour for company, gazed at the drifting sheets of rain and wondered whether it would be giving too much trouble to ask Mrs Birk to substitute a fire for the ferns and crinkly paper in the fireplace. Early in the afternoon Eugenia and Mrs Lace joined them and they all gloomed together. The labour of weeks, the excited expectation as it seemed of a lifetime, were being balked of an object before their very eyes; they felt hopelessly dejected.

'There is the squash court,' Eugenia muttered, without much conviction. Besides, the dress-rehearsal, which had taken place the day before, had been an utter failure in every respect, and everyone had been unanimous in deciding that it was essential to have another, but, of course, this was now impossible.

Conversation progressed in snatches, by common consent all pretended to take it for granted that tomorrow would be fine.

'Mr Wilkins must remember to take off his hat, or bow, or something to the cheering populace. He sat right back and one couldn't see him at all.'

'I thought he was just wonderful,' said Lady Marjorie.

'Besides, I think he ought to sit on the left-hand side, so that he can get out first and hand out Mrs Lace.'

'Noel is handing me out,' said Mrs Lace.

'Eugenia, if you can remember, do tell the coachman to drive at foot's pace, after all, we must try and make the arrival really impressive, it is far the most important episode. To my mind everything depends on how that goes off.'

'Didn't you think the platform looked rather bare? I thought it might be hung with flags or something to cheer it up a bit.'

'Union Jacks,' said Eugenia, 'I will see to that.'

'The first messenger must be very strictly told not to approach the platform until little Margaret Cooper has finished presenting her bouquet to Queen Charlotte. All that part was so fearfully rushed yesterday.'

'I think myself that we ought to have the Morris dancing first, before the episodes begin.'

'That's not a bad plan, but if we do we mustn't forget to tell Miss Trant.'

'And Mr Wilkins.'

'Oh, this rain!'

'You know the episodes do vary frightfully. I thought the Boston Tea Party was a pretty good flop myself.'

'Well, of course it was. None of the principals turned up for it you see and Miss Trant had to read all their parts in turn, so I suppose it was bound to be rather dreary.'

'Anyway it was exactly like *Alice in Wonderland* – and always will be.'

'Who is responsible for the Boston Tea Party?'

'The Barton branch,' said Eugenia, 'and I had a letter this morning from their leader saying that their charabanc broke down on the way here. It will be mended by tomorrow. I say, Union Jackshirt Aspect, can't you make Mr Wilkins speak up in the: "Leave our great Empire then, vile democrats" speech at the Boston T.P. It is a frightfully important speech and he mumbled it dreadfully.'

'I thought he was just wonderful,' said Lady Marjorie. 'Oh, dear! how divine he looked in his robes too.'

'Oh, this rain!'

'One thing,' said Eugenia, 'if it rains an inch tomorrow we do get £100 out of the insurance.' Jasper had arranged this transaction, gaining a small commission for himself in the process. 'We'll get that anyhow,' he said, 'it is going to be measured in the schoolmaster's rain gauge and I thought of nipping round there with a small watering can some time during the day.'

'You know, Jasper, something must be done about Nelson's arm, so that it doesn't show. Yesterday one could see it under the pinned-up sleeve all the time, it did look so idiotic.'

'Yes, and why does Nelson limp and pretend to be deaf? Gross overacting, I call it.'

'Of course the whole Nelson episode is a bit unsatisfactory. For instance, was Lady Hamilton really so matey with George the Third? I have a sort of idea she was never received at Court at all, and anyway he was batty by then.'

'Nobody will know that.'

'Well, I dare say, but I'm sure everyone knows she wasn't at Nelson's death-bed. There is a very famous picture of it for one thing.'

'She isn't *meant* to be in it,' cried Jasper despairing, 'I've told her time and again to keep off. She quite ruins the "Kiss me, Hardy" bit.'

'Oh! but what happened yesterday was that Hardy never turned up, and as somebody had to kiss the old boy, Lady Hamilton did seem to be the obvious person.'

'It appears she's nuts about him, in real life, I mean. Miss Trant told me.'

'Anyway, I saw a letter in the *Sunday Times* saying it was really Kismet, Hardy.'

'I don't care, Hardy kissed him all right. Everybody knows that.'

'Oh, this rain!'

'Didn't you think the bit where Wolfe recites Gray's "Elegy" to his troops dragged rather? I suppose it couldn't be pruned at all?'

'And Napoleon on board the *Bellerophon* looked exactly like the "Wounding of Nelson at the Canary Islands". I told you it would.'

'It struck me that Napoleon was blind, anyway.'

'Well, I don't know where he found anything to drink, I never did.'

'The ennobling of Pitt was nice,' said Eugenia. 'I must tell the Comrades to cheer like anything for that. Had Pitt been alive today he would have been a Social Unionist, of course. So would Fox.'

'Oh, this rain!'

'By the way,' said Eugenia, 'one of the old carriage horses has gone quite lame since yesterday, so we are going to use Vivian Jackson instead. He is awfully pleased, the darling, he loves to be in on things.'

The rain continued all the evening without a break. It poured and poured. At tea-time the telegram Jasper had sent his sister returned to him, 'Gone abroad, whereabouts not known'.

'Oh, dear,' he said gloomily, 'it never rains but it pours. I suppose when cheques begin coming back on one it is quite natural for telegrams to follow suit. I say old boy, lend me ten pounds.'

'Sorry, old boy.'

'Darling Miss Smith,' he said, much later in the evening, 'are you going to marry me or aren't you? I should be glad to know soon.'

'Why?'

'Because if not I think I shall bunk after the pag.'

'Where to?'

'Uruguay.'

'Oh, I wouldn't do that.'

'Then marry me.'

'I will tell you tomorrow,' said Poppy, 'after the pageant is over – if it ever takes place at all. Oh, this rain!'

Jasper wondered why he found it impossible to borrow ten pounds from Poppy. He had never been troubled by such diffidence before in his relations with women. Poor little Marigold, indeed, had once been left in pawn in a Paris hotel where he had found it impossible to pay the bill, and for all he knew she was still there. He could not quite imagine himself meting out such treatment to Poppy.

'Good night, darling,' he said, 'oh, this rain!'

There was but little sleep in the Jolly Roger that night, the weather was too much on everybody's mind. Some composed themselves for rest with their curtains drawn back so that they could observe from their beds the smallest change, others tried to forget their anxiety by shutting the windows, but soon found themselves making continual pilgrimages to open them again. At 2 a.m. the rain suddenly stopped and except for the regular dripping of trees there was no sound. The sky could not be seen, or any stars, there was a profound darkness. Shortly before five o'clock advancing daylight revealed that the village was wrapped in an opaque white mist. At eight o'clock this began to clear, and by nine a hot sun was pouring down its rays on to the steamy fields. It was a perfect summer day.

17

It was a perfect summer day. Morning sun blazed into the windows of the Jolly Roger, but quite failed to awaken the occupants. As soon as they felt perfectly confident that this fine weather was an indisputable fact, they had all made up for a wakeful night by sinking into happy, carefree slumber. The more the sun shone the sounder they slept. It was not until nearly eleven o'clock, when Eugenia and Vivian Jackson appeared on Chalford green, that they were finally aroused by a hideous din, compounded of shouting, neighing, and the cracking of a whip. Sleepy faces appeared, one by one, in four windows.

'Hail! and arise, Union Jackshirt Comrades!' cried Eugenia. 'I don't know how you could still be in bed on such a day – I myself have been out since dawn. There is much work for all to do in Chalford Park – I command you, as your district leader, to follow me there without delay.' She dragged Vivian Jackson's head right round, whereupon he reared twice and gave several tremendous buck-jumps, after which he galloped away, while Eugenia, sitting like a rock, sang at the top of her voice, 'Land of Union Jackshirts, Mother of the Flag'.

Poppy was the first to be ready. She abandoned her usual post in the battle of the bathroom, having had the wily idea that it might be possible to take a hot, deep bath in Chalford House whilst dressing for the pageant. She came downstairs delighted at having thus stolen a march on the others. On the hall table she saw, for the first time since she had been at the Jolly Roger, a letter addressed to herself. And, what was more, addressed in the once loved and always familiar handwriting of Anthony St Julien. She felt a little giddy as she opened it.

It was, for him, a long letter, four pages of writing which began by being small and neat and which ended up large and untidy. In it he suggested that Poppy should return to him at once. He said that his house was getting very uncomfortable, the cook had given notice and the housemaid, although he reminded her daily, either could not or would not send the loose covers to be cleaned. He considered too, that the weekly books were over large. He then went on to say, towards the end of the second page, that no other woman would ever mean much in his life, and that if she was prepared to let bygones be bygones he would be glad to welcome her home again. No direct reference to the detectives or the débutante. Poppy wondered what she would do. Anthony St Julien was, after all, her husband, and she loved her little house in Chapel Street. She did not have to close her eyes in order to visualize her drawing-room with its trellis wall-paper, red plush-curtains and satinwood furniture. It would be much harder to leave a dwelling to which she was singularly devoted, than a husband for whom devotion was now a thing of the past. In a position in which many women would be weighing an old loyalty against a new passion, she found herself wondering whether it would be possible to smuggle her writing-table out of the house, should she decide to throw in her lot with Mr Aspect. This indecision in no way troubled her, she felt sure that once the Grand Union Jackshirt Pageant and Garden Party was over she would with certainty know her own mind.

Noel also found a letter that morning. It was from one of the uncles and informed him that he should go to London as soon as might be, when an interview would be arranged for him with a Viennese banker who might be feeling disposed to offer him employment. He immediately sent off a telegram to the uncle saying that he would be in London the following day.

When all were ready, they packed into the motor car which kind Mr Birk had placed at their disposal, and were driven to Chalford Park. In and around the house a state of chaos reigned, it was hard to imagine that things would ever straighten themselves out. Workmen, Social Unionists, the Women's Institute and a multitude of reporters were falling over each other outside, whilst inside, Miss Trant and Mrs Lace were engaged in a battle royal over dressing-rooms. Fourteen large bedrooms had been placed at their disposal for this purpose by Lady Chalford, and Mrs Lace was insisting that she would need, in order to dress those appearing in the Chalford episode, at least seven. As she was responsible for dressing twenty people, and as Miss Trant was expecting to have at least two hundred on her hands, it was felt that Mrs Lace's demands were disproportionate. Finally, after a long and enraged argument, Mrs Lace was persuaded to make do with three rooms only. These she now proceeded to deck out with finery, laying dresses all over the beds and chairs, and covering the tables with accessories. Jasper and Poppy wandered in to have a look, and concluded that Mrs Lace had sat for too long at the feet of the Rackenbridge young men. Her ideas on dressing up were very modern.

'I rather think,' said Jasper, in one of his loud asides, 'that these American-cloth kirtles, cardboard wigs and cellophane fichus are going to look very peculiar alongside the two hundred Dolly Varden and Dresden Shepherd dresses hired by darling Miss Trant from the Oxford costumier.'

'I say, they are ugly,' murmured Poppy, 'have I really got to wear this monstrosity of a wig?'

'It's your own fault, darling, you wouldn't take the trouble to get a dress for yourself and now you are at the mercy of Rackenbridge taste. Serves you right too.'

Lady Marjorie looked quite wild with excitement and ran about looking for Mr Wilkins, saying, 'I can't wait, I can't wait.' Mr Wilkins, however, had not yet appeared on the scene.

The morning passed in a flash.

Lady Chalford, who was thoroughly enjoying the unwonted bustle, begged that everybody would stay on for a cold luncheon, to which she had already invited the curator of Peersmont and his charges. The years seemed to have rolled away from her on this occasion; she looked like a young woman as she greeted her old friend the Duke of Driburgh and those two of his colleagues considered by the curator as suitable candidates for the days outing.

The Duke, however, slipped away from her side as soon as he decently could and made a bee-line for Poppy, whom he embarrassed considerably with his attentions. When luncheon-time came he manœuvred that she should sit next him, kept his knee clamped against hers during the entire meal and held her hand between the courses. When she tried to thank him for the tiara he ogled her fearfully and dropped a few mysterious hints.

'How is Lord Rousham?' she asked, to change the subject.

'Off his diet, I am sorry to say. Won't eat anything now, except the coco-nuts and bits of suet we put out for the tits. Gunnersbury is busy making a nesting box for him, meddling old idiot, he always has fussed over housing conditions, and so on. I've no patience with his silly socialistic ideas; if a man likes to build his own nest, let him. Trade Unions have been the downfall of this country you mark my words, young lady.'

After luncheon the duke led Poppy into the recess of a window and proposed marriage to her.

'But you're married already Duke,' she cried, in order to gain time. There was a wild look in his eye which she did not altogether like.

'Ah, you think I am old-fashioned, behind the times, eh, what? But I have been getting very modern in my outlook lately I can assure you, and I understand that nowadays it is perfectly usual to be engaged while one is still married. Damned sensible idea. Now I suggest that we should give old Maud all the evidence she wants and then we could nip round to a registry office. What do you say to that, little lady? There are lots more pretty toys hanging on the tree where that tiara came from, you know.'

'That will be lovely,' said Poppy, 'and now, Duke —'

'Call me Adolphus.'

'And now, Adolphus, I am really rather busy. If you will excuse me I think I should be going. But I will see you again soon.'

'And for good, little lady, for good,' cried the amorous Adolphus, leering after her.

Poppy, who had nothing whatever to do for at least another hour (they had lunched early and very quickly), escaped next door into the library, where she could hide herself from her admirer behind jutting-out bookcases. She was rather pleased to see that the daily papers were there, neatly arranged on a large round leather-topped table, and taking up *The Times* she began to glance through it in a desultory manner. Almost the first thing to meet her eye was the name of Anthony St Julien's débutante heading the list of marriage announcements; the girl was engaged to a well-known polo player.

Poppy now understood the eagerness with which Anthony St Julien wanted her back again; she felt sorry for him, but at the same time considered that his behaviour was unnecessarily crude. He might have waited for a day or two. At the same time she was rather grateful to him for having been so caddish, as now, whatever course she should decide to take, she would be not treating him otherwise than as he deserved. Her thoughts once more turned towards the writing-table. It was rather heavy, but she and Jasper between them could probably carry it out in the middle of the night.

Presently she was sought out by Lady Marjorie, who looked quite ghoulishly hideous in mauve panniers of American-cloth over a skirt of bright silver mackintosh. The wire-netting wig made for her by Mrs Lace had proved too small and very painful to wear, so she had cast it away, and borrowed instead a Dolly Varden one from Miss Trant. This was of very untidy white horse-hair, which stood up in a fuzzy aureole round her head; a corkscrew curl fell behind one ear, and became more of a corkscrew and less of a curl at every step she took. The wig was rather too large for Lady Marjorie and her own dark hair strayed out behind, in spite of innumerable hairpins.

'Gosh!' said Poppy, trying not to look horrified at this apparition, 'dressed already?'

'There's no need to be, for ages yet, but I wanted to get it over. I'm really too excited to sit still and wait.'

'I had to hide in here,' said Poppy, 'because that awful old duke pounced me. In fact, he went so far as to propose marriage.'

'Highty-tighty, awful old duke indeed. When I think of the way you always go on to me about Osborne. So I suppose you have accepted with pleasure – do I congratulate you, darling?'

'My darling Marge – *that* old duke?'

'Nonsense. He's a very nice old duke, much nicer than that mountain of pomposity you want me to marry. Darling, do I look all right?'

'Lovely, darling.'

'That's good. Because – you know – Mr Wilkins. I wanted to look quite my best on his account, the angel. Oh, dear! it does seem hard I can't drive in the coach with him.'

'Never mind, I really think you have a better chance of getting off with him like this, because you'll be sitting next him for hours on the platform, and when the episodes are over, Noel is going to escort the local beauty round the Olde Englyshe Fayre. That'll be your big opportunity.'

'Oh, I am excited! I keep feeling quite cold and shivery. The Social Unionists ought to be here any minute now in their chara-bancs. Do come and dress, Poppy, I feel too shy to go and look for Mr Wilkins by myself.'

Presently, to the accompaniment of Union Jackshirt songs, cheers and yells, the Comrades began to arrive. They appeared to be in the wildest of good spirits as they were shepherded by their district leaders into Miss Trant's dressing-rooms, where they proceeded to cover their Union Jack shirts with cotton brocade coats and sateen breeches, or cotton brocade panniers and sateen skirts, according to their sex. Made-up jabots of cheap lace were tied round their necks and frills of it sewn to their sleeves, but these did not fit very well and in most cases a few inches of red, white and blue were to be seen poking out. Jasper, hot and perspiring in one of Mrs Lace's artistic rubber suits, was taking his duties as producer with the utmost seriousness. He dashed about, a grubby piece of paper in one hand and megaphone in the other, admonishing the various district leaders and trying to make sure that all the groups had arrived upon the scene. Finally he stood on a chair and addressed them all through his megaphone.

'Now, boys,' he said, 'there are one or two little things I wish to mention. The dress-rehearsal on Monday did not go off too well. Nobody was dressed, and you could hardly have called it a rehearsal. However, that's not going to stop us from doing splendidly this afternoon. Now, I want you all to try and enter into the spirit of the age – remember, you are in the eighteenth century from now on. When the coach drives up with King George and Queen Charlotte in it, I want you all to be lining the drive – give them a good rousing cheer, don't yell and don't give the Social Unionist salute. Let a few words be audible: 'God bless His Majesty'; 'Long live the House of Hanover'; 'Queen Charlotte for ever', and so on, and as the coach passes, fall on one knee. Those of you whose wigs are not sewn on to your hats might snatch them off, the hats, I mean, and wave them. Another important point – remember, you will have plenty of time to get into your places for the episodes while the King and Queen are alighting and hearing speeches of welcome. On Monday you all scrambled far too much; there was an appalling muddle. Now I will read over the list of the episodes again in their proper order, as I want to get it all clear.

'Arrival of George the Third and Queen Charlotte (Union Jackshirt Wilkins and Mrs Lace).

'Speech of Welcome by Lord Chalford (Union Jackshirt Noel Foster).

'Answering speech by George the Third.

'Pause, for Morris dancing.

'First messenger arrives announcing the victory of Wolfe over French Pacifists at Quebec.

'*First Episode*: Wolfe, while reading Gray's "Elegy in a Country Churchyard" to his troops, is hit by a stray bullet and dies on a heap of straw. Rackenbridge brass band plays the "Dead March in Saul".

'Messenger arrives announcing the doings at the Boston Tea Party. Speech by George the Third "Leave our Great Empire then, vile democrats," etc.

  '*Second Episode*: The Burghers of Boston, with halters round their necks, pour their tea on the ground and drink illicit whisky instead. Rackenbridge brass band does *not* play the "Dead March in Saul", (as it did on Monday) but "Little Brown Jug Don't I Love Thee".

'Messenger arrives announcing that Clive and Warren Hastings have disgraced themselves in India.

  '*Third Episode*: Clive and Warren Hastings, seated on an elephant, are surrounded by Nautch girls – (by the way, I hope the hind legs is here this afternoon, Miss Trant had to be them on Monday – Ah! Union Jackshirt Pierpont, good). Rackenbridge brass band plays "In a Persian Garden".

  'Pause, for the ennobling of Pitt. Rackenbridge brass band plays "For he's a jolly good fellow".

'Messenger arrives announcing the French Revolution. Rackenbridge brass band plays "Mademoiselle from Armentières".

  'Another messenger arrives announcing the wounding of Nelson at the Canary Islands and his naval victory over French Pacifists.

  'Speech by George the Third. "God blew His breath and they were scattered", etc.

  '*Fourth Episode*: Nelson, his telescope pressed to his blind eye, and staring at Lady Hamilton with his other one, has his arm blown off. Rackenbridge brass band plays, "Every nice girl loves a sailor, every nice girl loves a tar". Tableau of Lady Hamilton in one of her attitudes.

'Messenger arrives announcing Death of Nelson.

  '*Fifth Episode*: Nelson dying on a heap of straw, Hardy kisses him. Speech by Nelson, "It is a far, far better thing I do", etc. Nelson dies saying, "Look after pretty witty Emmie". Rackenbridge brass band plays the "Dead March in Saul" again.

'Final tableau: "The Exile of Napoleon".
'Rackenbridge brass band plays "God save the King".

'I hope that is all quite clear to you now,' said Jasper, rather hoarsely, as he jumped down from his chair.

Meanwhile, the neighbourhood was turning up in force. Had T.P.O.F. only known it, her change of plans was to avail her nothing, and the very people whose presence beneath her roof was so obnoxious to her were all busily paying their shillings at the park gates. They were not only eager to enjoy this pageant, the advertisements of which had been so strangely worded, but most of them had long been immensely curious to see Eugenia, the unknown heiress, and the by now almost legendary beauties of Chalford House. Large shining cars therefore sailed up the drive one after another, to be directed by Comrades to a rather soggy parking-place where they disgorged the infamous *élite* of the neighbourhood. They all laughed and chattered together, crying out that the house was a dream and wondering whether they should meet Eugenia; the weight of shame lay lightly upon their shoulders – they would have been surprised if they knew the violence of Lady Chalford's feelings about them.

The hour of three was near at hand. Mrs Lace, resplendently 1927 in her gilded American-cloth dress and wig of paper-clips, had long ago disappeared with Mr Wilkins to a place behind the kitchen-garden, where the royal coach awaited them. The party of welcomers was gracefully posed round the front door, ready to greet the Sovereign and his Consort with elegant bows and curtsies; Beau Brummels, Scarlet Pimpernels and Lady Teezles lined the drive for as far as the eye could see, all agog to make a loyal eighteenth-century demonstration. The crowd of onlookers had assumed proportions such as nobody had dared to hope for.

A hush of expectation fell upon all.

'Something awful is going to happen,' said Jasper, nervously. 'I know it.'

At last thrilling cheers were heard, the coach was evidently on its way. A shudder of excitement swept the crowd, all necks were craned to see the great arrival, all breaths were drawn in to swell the cheering which was coming ever nearer. Suddenly it wavered, lost heart and stopped. A noise like thunder was heard instead, punctuated by horrible thin shrieks, and the next moment the coach came crashing into sight with horses at full gallop and evidently quite out of control. Mrs Lace, screaming loudly, was attempting to throw herself out of a window, and was being forcibly restrained from doing so by Mr Wilkins. Both their wigs had fallen off.

The crowd now took to its heels. It seemed as though nothing could save coach and horses from being dashed to pieces against Chalford House when suddenly, Mr Wilkins, having thrown Mrs Lace on to the floor, climbed out through the window and up on to the coachman's seat, where he wrenched the reins from the trembling and inefficient hands of Lady Chalford's ancient groom. In the nick of time he managed to drag Vivian Jackson and his colleague up onto the grass. The coach, after rocking frantically for a moment, overturned, and both horses were brought to a standstill. The Comrades now dashed forward; with ready hands they dragged forth the hysterical Mrs Lace, and carried away the groom on an improvised stretcher – he appeared to be suffering from concussion. Lady Marjorie, beside herself with love and admiration, implored her hero to tell her that he was still alive, which he did very heartily; Eugenia sobbed on the neck of her horse, 'Darling, darling Vivian Jackson, you must never frighten me like that again, you might have been killed. Are you sure you're all right?' She felt his legs one after the other and presently led him away to his loose-box.

'Funny thing,' said Mr Wilkins to Jasper, 'a chap who lives at Rackenbridge – forget his name – caused all the trouble. He sprang out of the crowd waving a yellow flag at the horses, extraordinary stupid thing to do, you know; why, they might easily have bolted.'

Mrs Lace was taken into Chalford House. Her golden gown was split in several places and her wig quite ruined but her person was unscathed. She indulged in a comforting exhibition of hysteria until Major Lace gave her a good shaking, after which she restored her face, borrowed a cotton-wool wig from kind Miss Trant, and resumed her place at the side of Mr Wilkins.

Meanwhile the pageant was proceeding as though nothing out of the way had happened. Mr Wilkins, perfectly unmoved by his shaking, remembered his speeches better than ever before and went through his royal part as to the manner born.

The Social Unionists gave him a rousing welcome as he mounted the platform.

'G.E.O.R.G.E! We want George!' they cried.

Lady Marjorie stood beside him, her horse-hair locks quivering, her heart thumping, her cheeks flushed. She also wanted George.

It was all an enormous success. The episodes went off without a single hitch and nobody seemed to notice the fact that Jasper had ignored historical truth to a degree unprecedented even in pageantry. The most popular scenes of all were just those with the smallest foundation in fact.

Social Unionists and the public alike shouted themselves to a frenzy when, a messenger arriving to tell George the Third that Louis of France had been razored up by Marxist non-Aryans, the English monarch observed sadly, 'Alas! my poor brother!'

The episodes were to have been brought to an end by a tableau representing Napoleon on board the *Bellerophon*, but at the last moment Eugenia had vetoed this, as it had suddenly occurred to her that, even though Napoleon was a dirty foreigner, he was nevertheless somebody's Leader. They ended therefore, rather pointlessly, with the Death of Nelson, which was not altogether a success from Jasper's point of view, as both Hardy and Lady Hamilton made an unseemly rush to kiss the expiring admiral. The public, however, appeared to enjoy it.

After this the Rackenbridge brass band struck up the tune of 'Onward, Christian Soldiers', to which the Social Unionists, standing at attention, sang their hymn.

'Onward, Union Jackshirts
Fight for England's fame.
Fight and die for England,
Saving her from shame.
When foreigners make grimaces,
Stamp them in the mud,
Jump upon their faces,
Cover them with blood.
Onward, Union Jackshirts
Fight for England's fame,
Fight and die for England,
Saving her from shame.

'Onward, Union Jackshirts
England shall win through.
England shall rise greater,
Thanks to Jackshirts true.
Junket fronts shall quiver,
We shall give them more
Reasons to shiver
Than they had before.
Onward, etc.

'Fight with shell and bullet,
Fight with castor oil,
Fight with pen and paper,
Fight, Oh Jackshirts loyal.
Fight the loathly Pacifist,
Fight the junket breast,
Make them feel the Jackshirt's fist,
Make them howl for rest.

Onward, Union Jackshirts
Foreigners you'll whack.
Fight and die for England
And the Union Jack.'

After this another unrehearsed incident took place. There was a moment's pause while George the Third prepared to descend from the platform for his inspection of the Olde Englyshe Fayre. The Comrades, who had completely entered into the spirit of the thing, were crowding round him cheering themselves hoarse, when suddenly and most unexpectedly they were attacked from the rear by quantities of horrible-looking men dressed as the *sansculottes* of Revolutionary France and wearing yellow caps on their heads. 'We want peace! we want peace!' they cried, scattering white feathers in every direction.

We will fight
Red, White and Blue
'Cos we are yellow
Through and through
We'll have a crack
At Captain Jack
Because we think
His heart is black.

'Kill Social Unionism!' and they fell upon the defenceless Comrades with life preservers, knuckledusters, potatoes stuffed with razor blades, bicycle bells filled with shot, and other primitive, but effective, weapons. The Social Unionists, who were not only unarmed, but also sadly hampered by their full-bottomed coats, ill-fitting breeches and the wigs, which in many cases fell right over their eyes, impeding their vision, were at first utterly overcome by the enemy. Many were laid out, others, less fortunate, were carried away to a distant part of the estate where atrocities too horrible to name were perpetrated upon their persons. Mrs Lace was dragged to the lake and there was soundly ducked more than once by masked, but vaguely familiar assailants.

Eugenia, meanwhile, had gone into the house to fetch a sunshade for her grandmother. On hearing the din of battle she rushed out again, to be confronted by an appalling scene of carnage. The Social Unionists, in small, scattered groups, were defending themselves bravely enough, but to no avail. They were completely disorganized, and it was clear that the Pacifists must win the day, unless something quite unforeseen should happen to turn the tide of war against them.

It happened. Like a whirlwind, Eugenia Malmains dashed into the fray, seizing a Union Jack from off the platform she held it high above her head and with loud cries she rallied the Comrades to her. The Pacifists fell back for a second in amazement, never had they seen so large, so beautiful, or so fierce a woman. That second was their undoing. They returned ferociously enough to the charge, but from now onwards the fight began to go against them. The Social Unionists, all rallying to Eugenia, presented at last a united front. Led by her, they shouted their fighting cry: 'We defend the Union Jack.'

> 'We will whack
> And we will smack,
> And we will otherwise attack
> All traitors to the Union Jack.
> For we defend the Union Jack.'

and charged again and again into the ranks of the enemy, which were gradually falling away before their determined onslaught. The cowardly Pacifists, armed to the teeth though they were, could stand up to the Jackshirt's fists no longer. They began to retire in extreme confusion, which ended in an utter rout. They fled, leaving in possession of the Comrades a battlefield on which were scattered a quantity of white wigs, white feathers and wounded men.

'How wonderfully realistic that was,' said Lady Chalford,

appreciatively. 'One might almost believe that some of those poor fellows were actually hurt.' She surveyed the scene through her lorgnettes, and addressed the Duke of Driburgh, who stood at her side. 'Mr Aspect,' she continued, 'has evidently inherited all your talent for writing, my dear Driburgh – I have never forgotten the pretty Valentines you composed so charmingly in those days.'

'Very kind of you, my dear,' said the Duke. 'I presume that what we have just witnessed is the Battle of Waterloo, with your dear little Eugenia in the part of Boadicea, such a clever notion.'

The Social Unionists, in spite of their wounds (and hardly one had escaped injury) now went quite mad with excitement. They hoisted Eugenia upon their shoulders and carried her, with loud cheers, to the platform, from which point of vantage she made a stirring speech. She urged that all who had witnessed this cowardly attack upon the peaceful Social Unionists should join their party without more ado. 'We are your only safeguard against Pacifism in its most brutal form,' she cried; 'do you want your streets to run with blood, your wives to be violated and your children burnt to death? No? Then join the Union Jack defenders here and now —' She pointed to her tattered flag, saying that in time it would surely be one of the most honoured relics of the Movement. She told the Comrades that their scars were honourable scars, received on a great occasion and in defence of a great cause. Their names would go down to history, she said, and become famous; they would boast in after years to their children and their children's children that they had been privileged to fight beneath the Union Jack in the Battle of Chalford Park.

This speech was received with the utmost enthusiasm, not only by the Comrades themselves but by members of the public, many of whom now hastened to become recruited to the Social Unionist party, Eugenia herself pinning the little emblem to their bosoms. Such Pacifists as had fallen into their enemies' hands were presently led away and treated to enormous doses of 'Ex-Lax', the 'Delicious Chocolate Laxative', which was the only substitute for castor oil to be found in Nanny's medicine-chest.

The victims of Pacifist atrocities now began to stagger back one by one. They told hair-raising tales of the treatment which they had received, and were hailed as martyrs and heroes by Eugenia, who wrote their names down in a small exercise book. When their wounds had been dressed, and the more serious cases had been put to bed in Lady Chalford's spare rooms (her ladyship having by this time retired, fatigued by the day's excitements to her own), Eugenia, at Jasper's suggestion, led a contingent of Social Unionists to the cellar, and several cases of vintage champagne were carried on to the lawn.

The Olde Englyshe Fayre from now on became more like an Olde Englyshe Orgy. An enormous bonfire was made, on which Karl Marx and Captain Chadlington (the local Conservative Member of Parliament) were burnt together in effigy amid fearful howls and cat-calls from the Comrades. 'Down with the Pacifists! Down with the Communists! Down with non-Aryans! Down with the Junket-fronted National Government! – We defend the Union Jack, we will whack and we will smack and we will otherwise attack all traitors to the Union Jack —'

Everybody danced with everybody else, some people even danced alone, certain sign of a good party, while the Rackenbridge brass band moaned out 'Night and Day', it's latest number, for hours on end. The visitors from Peersmont became as drunk as the lords they were, and, each with a pretty girl on his arm, refused to budge when the curator said that it was time to go home. Lady Marjorie and Mr Wilkins disappeared together for a while; when they rejoined the throng of merry-makers it was to dance a jig and announce their engagement. The Comrades cheered and sang their Union Jackshirt songs until they could cheer and sing no more, and it was not before one o'clock in the morning that they finally packed themselves into their charabancs and drove away, hoarse but happy.

Silence at last fell upon the park. Under a full moon Poppy and Jasper staggered hand in hand towards the Jolly Roger. In spite of their extreme exhaustion they still went on talking over the events of that sensational afternoon.

'Did you adore the fight?' asked Poppy; 'I did. I dug my heel into a fallen Pacifist's face – remind me to tell Eugenia that, by the way. It ought to give me a leg up in the Movement. And what were you up to? I never saw you.'

'No,' said Jasper, 'because I was hiding underneath the platform all the time. I can't bear being hurt.'

'Darling Jasper, you never let one down for a moment, do you?'

'Are you going to marry me?'

'Honestly, I don't see how I can help it. It would seem a bit wasteful not to keep you about the place, considering that you are the only person I've ever met who makes me laugh all the time without stopping.'

'Good,' said Jasper, 'we'll sell the tiara then, shall we?'

'Yes, darling!'

'And go to Uruguay next week?'

'No, darling. I shouldn't fancy that – fuzzy wuzzies aren't at all my dish!'

18

A large luncheon-table was prepared in the Iolanthe room at the Savoy. There were a great many glasses on it and a huge bouquet of orchids, while several champagne bottles in buckets of ice completed an atmosphere of extreme gaiety. The room next door was also thrown open and a cocktail-bar here awaited the assembling of the guests. All was now in readiness for the wedding luncheon-party of Mr Wilkins and Lady Marjorie Merrith, who were busy uttering nuptial vows in the presence of their nearest and dearest at the Caxton Hall, Westminster.

The first guest strayed into Iolanthe and thence into the next room, where she refused a cocktail which was pressed upon her by several waiters, but fell with healthy appetite upon the salted almonds and potato crisps. It was Eugenia, who, having given T.P.O.F. the slip, had found her way to London by an early train, and from thence to the Union Jack House, where she had spent a blissful morning with Comrades of the London branch. Her eyes still sparkled from excitement at the memory of her reception. The Captain had himself granted her an interview, warmly thanked her for all the work she had done on behalf of the Movement and had finally, as a token of gratitude, plucked, like the pelican, his own little emblem from his own bosom and pinned it, still warm, upon hers. When she had left the great man, tears of emotion streaming from her eyes, the Comrades had clustered round her and had made her give her own account of the now epic Battle of Chalford Park. After this they had made much of her, fed her on sausage rolls and twopenny bars, given her a special cheer and salute, and had all promised to visit the Chalford Branch in the nearest of futures.

As Eugenia was still wearing her usual costume of Union Jack shirt, old grey woollen skirt, belt complete with dagger, and bare legs and head, she cut a sufficiently incongruous figure in the sophisticated atmosphere of a large hotel. The waiters stared at her in astonishment and she returned their glances quite unabashed; she was lacking in the nervousness which many a young girl might have felt while spending her first day in London.

Presently Mrs Lace came trailing in, wearing clothes reminiscent of the riding habit of a widowed queen-empress. She also had been unable to attend the marriage ceremony, having spent her morning in a frenzied rush round the shops. Eugenia had already seen her that day, they had come up from Rackenbridge by the same train, the Laces travelling first-class and Eugenia third.

'Oh! how are you?' said Mrs Lace. For the hundredth time she took in the details of Eugenia's attire with a kind of disgusted satisfaction, disgust that one so rich should put her money to so little use, satisfaction that Eugenia would certainly never rival herself as the best-dressed woman in the Cotswolds. Eugenia, who could not understand the significance of her glances, thought that Anne-Marie was looking more grumpy than usual today. Presently, gathering up her velvet train, Anne-Marie sauntered to a looking-glass, where she rearranged her silver fox to its best advantage and pinned to it a couple of gardenias which she took out of a thick white paper bag. She looked at herself with her head on one side and her lips pursed as though she were about to whistle, after which she swayed back to the side of Eugenia, who was happily browsing in a basket of crystallized fruits.

'Cold, isn't it?' said Mrs Lace, in her foreign accent. In truth, she was not feeling quite happy about her black velvet, furs and feathers; the day being a particularly hot one in late September, she was beginning to wonder whether she was not rather unsuitably dressed for it. 'Cold, isn't it?'

'No,' said Eugenia, with her mouth full.

'I always think these autumn days singularly deceptive, they look so warm, but one has to be very careful, *le fond de l'air est cru.*'

'It's perfectly boiling today,' said Eugenia, scornfully. 'I don't know what those foreign words mean I'm afraid. Under the régime people will talk English or hold their tongues.'

'My dear child, how ridiculous you are. Régime itself is a French word, you know.'

'Oh! no, it's not,' said Eugenia, 'it has become anglicized long ago by the Comrades.'

Jasper and Noel now came in. Jasper flung his arms round Eugenia's neck. 'You simply can't have any idea how pleased I am to see you, darling,' he cried 'I never thought you would make it.'

'Nor did I,' said Eugenia. 'Luckily T.P.O.F. is ill in bed, so she will never know, unless that old yellow Pacifist of a Nanny tells her. I rode to the station on Vivian Jackson and had to leave him tethered there all day, the poor angel.'

'Well, and what have you been up to since we left?'

'Oh! nothing much, it's been fairly dull down there (you heard we made a hundred and eighty-six pounds for the Movement, I suppose?) But today has been wonderful. I was able to keep a non-Aryan family from getting into my carriage at Oxford simply by showing them my little emblem and drawing my dagger at them and I can't tell you what a morning I've had with the Comrades at the Union Jack House – Oh, boy!'

'Come next door and let's hear about it,' said Jasper, mischievously, leaving Noel to a tête-à-tête with Mrs Lace.

Noel was now wondering whether he had ever really been in love with her at all. Good manners, however, demanded that he should keep up the fiction, so he kissed her hand, gazed passionately into her eyes and murmured that he was happy to be with her again.

'*Moi aussi je suis contente*,' said Mrs Lace, with a mournful look. She felt that her black velvet, if rather sweaty in such weather, at least assisted her to present a highly romantic appearance. 'How are things going with you, *mon cher*?' She had been cheated out of her great renunciation scene at Chalford, perhaps she would be able to enact it here and now.

'I am rather worried,' said Noel, snatching at any opportunity to talk about himself as opposed to themselves. The others could not now be long in coming, until they did, the conversation must be kept on a safe level. He cursed Jasper for leaving them together, typical piece of spitefulness. 'I am doubtful now whether I shall get that appointment in Vienna I told you of. My uncle, who has some influence there, is still trying hard to get it for me, and General von Pittshelm, an old friend of my parents, is pulling certain strings, I believe. All the same, it seems fairly hopeless – so much stands in the way.'

On hearing this Mrs Lace felt thankful that things had gone no farther between herself and Noel. She had begun to think during the calm, dull weeks which had succeeded the pageant that the penniless heir to a throne, which he was unlikely ever to ascend, would be a poor exchange for the solid comforts of the Lace home, although he might provide a sweet romance to while away a boring summer. It behoved her to be discreet.

'You never came to say goodbye to me,' she murmured, plaintively.

'Darling, it wasn't possible. If you only knew —'

'I think I do. We must say goodbye here, then, I suppose. In public. It seems hard.'

'But I shall come to Chalford again awfully soon, you know.'

'It can never be the same. My husband – he knows something of our romance and suspects more. I have had a terrible time since you left.'

'I say, not really? Is he – will he – I mean he hasn't got anything on us, has he?'

'My husband,' said Mrs Lace, grandiloquently, 'will forgive me everything. He has a noble character and moreover he loves me to distraction.'

'Thank heaven!' said Noel, 'I mean – you know, darling, that I would love to carry you right away from Chalford for ever, but it isn't possible in the circumstances. I am much too poor. Besides, I could never have taken you from your children; the thought of them would have come between us in the end. All the same, I shall love you for ever; you will always be the love of my life.'

'And you,' said Mrs Lace, 'of mine.'

She looked up at him with her sideways glance that she supposed to be so alluring, and thought, as she used to think when he first came to Chalford, that his was an unromantic appearance. 'More like a stockbroker than a king,' she thought.

'If you should ever happen to be passing through Vienna,' he was saying, 'you must look me up, if I go, and we will do the night-clubs together if there are any, although I hear it is far from gay there now. A friend of mine who has just come back from there tells me that he is off to North Wales in search of amorous adventure – been reading Caradoc Evans, I suppose.

'Ah!' he cried, greatly relieved, 'here come the others at last.'

A buzz of lively conversation could be heard approaching down the corridor. Mrs Lace took up a position by the window, twitching at her fox. She opened her eyes very wide and assumed an expression of romantic gloom.

The door burst open. Lady Marjorie, radiant and beautiful in white crêpe-de-chine with a huge black hat, appeared hand in hand with Mr Wilkins. She looked the very picture of happiness. Mr Wilkins looked the same as usual, except for his smart grey suit and buttonhole of a red carnation. Immediately after them came Lady Fitzpuglington, escorted by a well-known statesman and followed by a flock of smart and glittering young people, which included Poppy St Julien.

Lady Fitzpuglington, considering what her feelings must have been on the subject, had behaved extraordinarily well to Marjorie over this marriage. She had made three earth-shaking scenes about it, after which, seeing that nothing she could say would avail to alter the girl's determination, she had given way with a good grace, merely stipulating that the wedding itself should be kept absolutely private, in order that the Duke of Dartford's feelings might be spared as far as possible.

'There's nothing to be done,' she told her brother. 'Marjorie is of age and madly in love, therefore nothing I can say or do will stop her. We must make the best of a bad job and be thankful that divorce is such an easy matter in these days. Poor Mr Wilkins, of course, doesn't want to marry her in the least, but there it is, poor man. Now, if Puggie had only taken my advice and left her a minor until the age of forty, how different it would all have been. We should at least have had some hold over the little idiot then.'

Her ladyship's brother did not reply. He thought that the unlucky Fitzpuglington, floating as he had been, a six months corpse in the Atlantic when his daughter was born, might be excused for having failed to provide against her passion for Mr Wilkins. Lady Fitzpuglington was noted in the family as being an adept at loading her own responsibilities upon the shoulders of other people.

Mrs Lace noticed that the ladies of the party were not curtsying to Noel even his hostess had not greeted him. She found this puzzling. Surely in London he did not preserve his incognito. Also she was very much annoyed when she saw that the other young women present were every bit as pretty as she. She thought their clothes excessively boring, however. They were all of the plainly tailored variety, consisting of little suits or crêpe-de-chine dresses covered by thin woollen coats. Mrs Lace only cared for fancy dress. She wished, all the same, that she had put on something a trifle cooler, she was boiled in her riding habit.

'I say, darling,' whispered one of the pretty ladies to Marjorie, 'is that a fortune-teller over by the window, or what? And who is that lovely mad-looking girl with no hat?'

Major Lace now appeared. He had been best man to his friend and had only just got away from the registry office. Mrs Lace, for once in her life, was pleased to see her husband. In all this large gay crowd nobody was paying any attention to her; she almost felt that she would be glad to be back in Chalford again where she was the undisputed belle.

'Are you going to marry Union Jackshirt Aspect?' Eugenia asked Poppy.

'Yes darling, I am, isn't it wonderful. My husband was rather tiresome about it at first, but now he's really behaving quite well and I think, with any luck, he ought to let me divorce him.'

'Why?' asked Eugenia.

'Well, it's not usual for ladies to be divorced, you know, my sweet, and the old boy has always been a great one for etiquette. Those detectives were never anything to do with him at all, just down there for a hol. we found out afterwards. Awfully funny, really, when one thinks of it. Will you come to my wedding, Eugenia?'

'I will, and we'll have a Social Unionist guard of honour, if you like. I hope you will be very happy, Cousin Poppy St Julien, and continue to work for the Cause after your marriage.'

At luncheon Jasper and Noel sat one on each side of Mrs Lace.

'By the way old boy,' Jasper said to Noel, leaning across her, 'I don't want that job of yours any more. Poppy and I got forty thousand pounds for the tiara, you know, and I think of standing for Parliament or something like that as soon as the divorce is over. It occurred to me that if your Viennese business doesn't come off as you hope, you might care to go back to Fruel's. Sir Percy seems quite anxious to have you there again. I went to see him yesterday about a few investments I am making.'

'Too kind of you,' said Noel.

Faint suspicions, shadowy doubts which had long been gathering in Mrs Lace's mind were thus rudely confirmed. She would not, however, allow her brain to take in the full-portent of all this until she was safely in her first-class carriage, alone with Major Lace. Then she cried and cried. Major Lace supposed that she was in the family way again. She was.

Afterwards, Jasper said to Noel, 'Was it tactless of me to mention Fruel's like that? It occurred to me, too late, that perhaps you would really feel safer if she thought you were abroad?'

'She seems just about as ready to wind it all up as I am. I do think girls are queer.'

'Perhaps she has found out something to your discredit.'

'I don't suppose any such thing,' said Noel, peevishly.

'Bit tired of you perhaps?'

'Certainly not. The girl is madly in love with me, madly, but the husband has been cutting up rough and all that, and naturally she can't face leaving the children.'

'That must be a great relief for you, old boy.'

After luncheon the elder statesman made a speech proposing the health of bride and bridegroom. It was a long speech with rather poor jokes distributed like sugar plums here and there. Lady Marjorie replied to it, as Mr Wilkins was too bashful. She said that it was fearfully kind of everybody to give her a second lot of wonderful wedding presents so soon after having the first ones returned. The second ones were much the nicest, too. She was fearfully happy, she said, inconsequently, and indeed this was apparent to all beholders. She hoped that everybody would come to her house warming party when she and Mr Wilkins had returned from their honeymoon and settled in Carlton House Terrace, where she had bought a house. 'In fact, you can all come and stay if you like,' she added, 'as we shall have quantities of spare rooms.'

'Good,' said Jasper, '"where I drinks I sleeps" has always been my favourite motto.'

Eugenia was now called upon, and leapt to her feet without the smallest diffidence, amid ringing cheers. She said that she was sure nobody could grudge any amount of gorgeous wedding presents to such a heavenly person as Lady Marjorie, or to such a brave Union Jackshirt as Mr Wilkins. In any case they certainly took with them on their honeymoon any amount of good wishes from herself and all the members of the Chalford Branch. As for the spare rooms, she said, it was to be hoped that they would soon be quite filled up with healthy little Aryan babies. The company then rose at her suggestion and sang:

> 'Land of Union Jackshirts,
> Mother of the Flag.'

★

Two days later Noel was back once more in the office of Fruel and Whitehead. Miss Brisket, Miss Clumps and Mr Farmer sat as of old in their appointed places. Noel was just coming to the end of a long telephone conversation. 'No, I'm sorry,' he was saying, in a firm and final voice, 'not sufficiently attractive.'

ALSO BY NANCY MITFORD

THE BLESSING

When Grace Allingham, a naïve young Englishwoman, goes to live in France with her dashingly aristocratic husband Charles-Edouard, she finds herself overwhelmed by the bewilderingly foreign cuisine and the shockingly decadent manners and mores of the French. But it is the discovery of her husband's French notion of marriage—which includes a permanent mistress and a string of casual affairs—that sends Grace packing back to London with their "blessing," young Sigismond, in tow. While others urge the couple to reconcile, little Sigi—convinced that it will improve his chances of being spoiled—applies all his juvenile cunning to keeping his parents apart. Drawing on her own years in Paris and her long affair with a Frenchman, Mitford elevates cultural and romantic misunderstandings to the heights of comedy.

Fiction/978-0-307-74083-0

DON'T TELL ALFRED

Fanny Wincham—last seen as a young woman in *The Pursuit of Love* and *Love in a Cold Climate*—has lived contentedly for years as housewife to an absent-minded Oxford don, Alfred. But her life changes overnight when her beloved Alfred is appointed English Ambassador to Paris. Soon she finds herself mixing with royalty and Rothschilds while battling her hysterical predecessor, Lady Leone, who refuses to leave the premises. When Fanny's tenderhearted secretary begins filling the embassy with rescued animals and her teenage sons run away from Eton and show up with a rock star in tow, things get entirely out of hand.

Fiction/978-0-307-74084-7

ALSO AVAILABLE:
Love in a Cold Climate, 978-0-307-74082-3
The Pursuit of Love, 978-0-307-74081-6

VINTAGE BOOKS
Available at your local bookstore, or visit
www.randomhouse.com